THE
MORE
A
THING
IS
PERFECT

The More a Thing is Perfect
Written by John H. Matthews
Copyright ©2020 John H. Matthews

ISBN: 978-1-970071-09-2

Library of Congress Control Number:
2020913569

This is a work of fiction. Names, characters, places, and incidents either
are the product of the author's imagination or are used fictitiously,
and any resemblance to actual persons, living or dead, business
establishments, events or locales is entirely coincidental.

Published by
Bluebullseye Press
A division of Bluebullseye LLC

Edited by Ginger Moran

Cover and book design
Copyright ©2020 John H. Matthews

Cover photo by Davide Ragusa

THE MORE A THING IS PERFECT

JOHN H. MATTHEWS

bluebullseye press

To

Brennan,

To sit on your

shelf, covered in dust,

while you live your own life

long after I'm

gone.

ALSO BY
JOHN H. MATTHEWS

Family Line
The South Coast
Ballyvaughan
Hangfire
Designated Survivor

Midway upon the journey of our life
I found myself within a forest dark,
For the straightforward pathway had been lost.

Ah me! How hard a thing it is to say
What was this forest savage, rough, and stern,
Which in the very thought renews the fear.

- Dante Alighieri, *Inferno*

CHAPTER ONE

Rust red terracotta tiles form jagged lines against the perfect blue sky of Florence. Scalloped edges zigzag their way across the artificial horizon, creating a contrast of colors that is both beautiful and stark.

The replica of Michelangelo's David presides over tourists with a sense of disinterest, slingshot over his shoulder, too consumed with thoughts of his battle yet to come to admire the scenery.

Florence is love and romance and seduction rolled into one. An aphrodisiac in shades of brown. If you visit the city not in love, you will be by the time you leave. Walk the stone streets and sip deep red wines sitting outside quiet cafés. Inhale the same air breathed by the masters of art and literature. Sleep naked with windows open as the hot Tuscan breeze flows over your bare skin.

The sky is always blue and the fields of Tuscany golden.

This is the ideal image of Italy, at least. The postcard view of romantics and dreamers, of a young Sophia Loren looking over her bare shoulder at you with a *What are you gonna do?* look in her eyes. It's staring at the muddy Arno flowing beneath you at sunset as men guide the long *barchetto* boats with amorous tourists on board, because no local would ever pay the fare. The smell of leather floats out of every other shop, fresh cappuccino from the ones in between them. And plenty of wine. Oh, the wine.

Come here in love, and this is the Florence you will experience. If you find love while here, it may reveal itself to you, as well. Sadly, most never experience it this way. Being in love and loving are two very different things. Italians understand this inherently, the difference between making love and fucking.

The mirage fades when you shake free of the love, the mystique you build up in your mind of the city for months while planning your dream trip, flipping through travel books that only show you the superficial, the overseen, the clichéd. For every famous sculpture there's a hundred just as beautiful. For every incredible view of the *Ponte Vecchio*, there's a hundred narrow streets with more charm and romance than all of the world combined.

I look across the piazza to the thousand tourists in cargo shorts and hometown high school football team T-shirts wearing oversized backpacks and carrying expensive cameras while taking photos on their iPhones so they can post them faster from café WiFi signals with hashtags like #bestvacayever, and #livingladolcevita. The illusion of romantic strolls, hand-in-hand with someone

I love, perhaps tasting each others gelato as we smile and giggle, fade quickly as I check to make sure my wallet hasn't already been lifted from my back pocket by a local thief eager to ruin a tourist's vacation. Maybe that is just me, jaded from my experiences, being here not in love.

Florence is an illusion. Look one way and it is perfection and beauty, the manifestation of a thousand years of lovers entering her. Turn around and it is the lower deck of a cruise ship, lined wall-to-wall with visitors seeking the cheapest souvenir replicas of Italian landmarks, T-shirts with tacky sayings and oversized pictures of the David's penis printed on them.

This is my second first impression of the city. My previous trip had been happier, and, yes, romantic. I did walk hand-in-hand with someone I loved. Her gelato was pistachio and stracciatella. Mine was dark chocolate and mixed berry. The tourists had been there but I never noticed them. They were a blur in my periphery that never came into focus. She was the only thing I cared to see and I saw the city only as an entity that surrounded her.

Her.

In my mind it should always be capitalized when referring to Her. We had almost six months together. A short time by most standards. Hell, by all standards except perhaps a first crush in junior high, destined to be over before you get to the point of holding hands without having sweaty palms, the feeling too new, sending hormones into pubescent overdrive. But it was six months full of fun and love and sex and laughter.

She was unexpected, but that's how they always say it happens. Look for love, you won't find it, but the moment you stop looking, there it is. BAM. I hadn't been looking for a long time. My work kept me occupied teaching during the day, writing at night. The time in between was filled with the mundane; grocery shopping, paying bills, deciding between the taupe and the beige towels for the guest bathroom that had never been used. Before her I was existing, going through the motions, miserable without the luxury of knowing it. I envy the people who recognize they're unhappy. They can confront it head on. Without that knowledge, you just think that's what life is supposed to be like, a daily drudge with no payoff. Better buy more milk. Flip through the take out menus from the kitchen drawer on Friday night like the Friday night before it, and the one before that. Lean against the trunk of the car while waiting for the gas pump to click off while inhaling the fumes a bit more than you should, just to dull the fucking pain. You get the idea.

I still don't think I was unhappy before her. Maybe just incomplete, as corny as that sounds. I have a nice house, a nice car, and a short commute. Everything is just…nice. There are enough friends in my radius so I'm not at home alone every weekend, but usually am by choice, or so I tell myself. Looking back, though, I can see the loneliness, the sadness. The wanting of something more. It isn't until after a life altering event that you can recognize a grown single man watching four hours of

HGTV every night while drinking grocery store merlot is a cry for help.

I'm not over her, and likely never will be. She wasn't my first love, but she filled a part of my life that has formed and shaped me into something else. Something more cynical, perhaps, but also someone that knows they are able to love and be loved. Before her I was content. With her I was happy. Without her, I don't know. Sad is too opposite to be accurate. I wouldn't say depressed, but there were certainly lingering moments late at night when I couldn't stop thinking about her, wishing I could call her, hear her voice one more time, feel the touch of her fingers on my skin again. Knowing something can be worse than not knowing. I'd had what I never imagined I would, then it went away. The memory of it will be with me forever, and so will the pain.

The first time I met her I was flustered and most likely began sweating immediately. I'd seen her sitting in the audience, a pleasant distraction from the usual attendees of my book readings. My eyes wandered to her more often than they should have, several times losing my place in the large printout version of my latest drivel of a children's mystery. A few parents turned to look at her, to see who kept pulling my attention. She had blushed and given a shrugging apology which only distracted me more for its perfection of motion.

I watched her come through the autograph line until she stood in front of me, a hand stuck out for an awkward handshake. She wore nice fitting jeans and a loose blouse that touched and pulled in the right places. Brown hair down, flowing across her shoulders. I'd looked up at her and momentarily lost the ability to speak. Then she did.

"I'm Olivia."

"Avery Gross," I said. It was instinct kicking in. I thought for a moment I could pull this off.

Her head tilted in confusion. I stared at her and wondered if I hadn't actually spoken, that no words had come from me, then realized what I'd done.

"I mean Hinton Chase."

She smiled and that had made me smile. I could smell her perfume and wondered what it was and wanted to smell it more, closer.

"So, you do use a pen name," she said.

"You blame me?"

She shrugged. "I like your real name."

"Then I'm Avery."

And she smiled the smile that would keep me warm for half a year.

That wasn't the first time I'd seen her. She'd been at my event downtown a couple weeks earlier, third row back, fourth seat from the left. I remembered such details because she stood out in the crowd of mothers wrangling the noisy and bored children that are my target audience. I didn't tell her I'd seen her before in case that would seem odd. Plus, I figured if I was going to have a stalker, I could do far worse than a 5 foot 6 inch dark haired beauty with a face that made me forget my own name. Or my fake name, as it was.

"Do you have a book for me to sign?"

"I…don't." And that smile.

Even I was smart enough to pick up on the signals and asked her out. We had drinks the next night and dinner downtown the following weekend. We spoke quietly over candlelight and laughed loudly, disturbing the elderly couple beside us celebrating an anniversary of unfathomable years. Our first kiss came after that dinner as we walked back to my car holding hands, followed an hour later by the first time we made love.

It was fast and wonderful. When she wasn't with me, I was nervous I wouldn't see her again. Beautiful, sweet, intelligent women don't show up in my life like she had. I was a pudgy thirty-five-year-old unmarried college professor that wrote children's books under a pseudonym. That's a difficult profile to match on Tinder.

We'd been together only three months when we were talking about the year she spent in Italy for college and how she wanted to go back. I had never travelled outside the states and said, "Let's do it." Perhaps it was the romantic moment, laying entwined in postcoital nudity, or the two bottles of wine we'd had before making love. But even as I said it, I wanted it to happen and began dreaming of eating gelato while walking across ancient squares with her.

I watched as she made the plans, compared flights, and read reviews on villas and apartments while narrowing down the places to visit. I'd given her my credit card and let her take care of everything. I dipped into my investment account to do it right. She was meticulous in her details, from wanting to make the most of her first trip back in more than ten years, to ensuring I enjoyed my first foray into European travel. The day finally came and we flew from Kansas City to JFK, then on to Florence.

I walk away from the piazza to flee the flocks of tourists. It's impossible to find a street with none, but at least you can minimize their numbers a bit. Most get jumpy when not in a pack and if you walk like you belong there, they will cross the street to avoid making eye contact.

Late into the evening, I sit at a café and drink wine while watching couples look into each other's eyes, and parents argue with children up well past their bedtimes from five time zones away.

Don't get me wrong, Florence is beautiful. It is perfect and flawed at the same time. But seeing it alone and out of love is an entirely different experience.

I shouldn't have come back to this city. I know that. The memories it left me with aren't romantic picture book moments. They are a stain; a burden. I want to see her again so badly, but know I can't. I felt drawn back, pulled, to see the places we'd seen together, eat the food, drink the wine again, and to look for answers, to try to find out why she'd died in our bed in Italy that night a year ago.

CHAPTER TWO

"Stand straight, arms to your sides." The tailor's thick accent commands me. I do as he says. The air in the small shop is heavy with the smell of cigarettes though no one is smoking. I wonder where a dry cleaner is to get the smell out before I wear the suit.

The three-way mirror shows the tan linen on my body, the jacket buttoned loosely over a white shirt open enough to show more of my pale chest than I'm comfortable with.

"Very niiiice," he says, seeming like a caricature with the extended word. Another pin is put in place. He checks my front. A hand moves up closer to my groin.

I was up early and jogged along the Arno River well before the tourists and even most locals were awake. I saw the morning sun hit the top of the large cathedral, the *duomo* that is the heart of the city, and felt special, like I was seeing something most people don't. It was a rare magical moment in the city for me this time around.

I'd returned home a year ago down 10 pounds and after a couple weeks of hiding in my house, decided I had to accept what had happened. That she was gone. I started walking, then jogging. After that came the gym with circuit training and weights. On the last trip I'd walked past the bespoke men's clothing shops with barely a glance at the beautiful suits in the windows. Today I'm buying one.

Our trip had been cut short when I returned home alone. Our relationship had happened so fast that hardly anyone knew I was dating someone, so there wasn't anyone to ask where she was. My parents live three hours away in Wichita and although I was eager to make that trip, to show off this amazing creature that loved being with me, I was hesitant as I knew my mother would begin the pressure for a wedding immediately. I only had to tell a lie to a few people from work when the fall semester started up again, that we'd broken up, she moved away, whatever it took. I saw the unsurprised looks in their eyes.

"You like here… or here…" The tailor offers two options for the cut of the slacks. I can't tell the difference between them.

"Whichever you like."

He grunts and slides another pin through the soft material. He sings while working. Through his accent I try to place the melody, working through the Italian classics in my mind before realizing it's a Taylor Swift song.

I glance in the mirror again. It barely looks like me. The $2,200 suit covers a lean and tan body. My salt and pepper beard, also a new addition in the last twelve months, was trimmed well by a barber here in the city when I first arrived a few days ago. Something catches my eye behind me in the reflection.

"May I try that on?" I turn to point.

The man sees another easy sale to add to the expensive suit and steps over to grab the hat. I reach for it and he motions to let me know he will put it on. He angles it, forehead first, an inch above the brow, then lowers the back.

Once placed on my head it seems to belong. The tightly woven two shades of brown straw form the shape of the fedora. A chocolate brown band wraps around the crown. It matches the suit perfectly. As he continues to mark the slacks with pins, I turn my head each way, eyeing the new addition to my persona. An embellishment. A lie, perhaps, for I'm not interesting enough to look this interesting. I imagine walking into my classroom back home, a couple dozen nervous freshmen in their first college course. Would they see this man and think, *hey, he must know his shit*. Or would they stifle laughter and talk about the dork they have for Lit.

I pay the man with euros out of my wallet, multiple crisp bills, counting them out slowly to ensure the fresh money wasn't sticking together, resulting in giving a bonus of a hundred euros or more. I see the amount left in my wallet diminished and know I'll need to visit the bank soon.

Out of the shop, I'm back in my clothes from Macy's which now feel overly incompetent. But I'm wearing the hat. The suit will take two days to alter so I have a couple more nights in Florence. It gives me time to go over my plans, which are mainly lists of places we'd been, where she and I had eaten and drank, where our lives intersected with the two named Pippo and Scarlet.

I'd spent the first six months crying for Olivia at night, sometimes clutching her pillow to my face, the faint smell of her lotions and perfume still emanating from the fabric, an olfactory ghost haunting me. Then I got pissed off. I started searching for news on Italian websites for any word of what happened to her, finding nothing. How could the death of an attractive young American woman in a foreign country go unnoticed?

My moods changed often during that time, and there were days I was sure the department head would call me in to release me from my teaching duties. I missed deadlines with my publisher and pissed off my agent. Then something would click and I'd be right with the world again, accepting what had happened and appreciating what time I'd had with her. In hindsight I recognize the signs of clinical depression. I know I needed to be seeing a shrink at the least and most likely should have been on meds, but there was no one to push me, to stage an intervention or beg me to go. I had isolated myself.

As I began to work out and take better care of myself, the moods stabilized, though one disorder was likely replaced with another. I was obsessed with finding out anything I could and spent many long nights searching websites and translating text to find any mention of her or the couple. I never called the police. That would have thrown a red flag over me I didn't need. It drove me to begin my plans to return.

I made notes and retroactively created a journal of our time here, tracked our movements, wrote down everywhere we'd eaten, drank, or made love. When I finished I realized how few days she and I had alone in Italy. The rest were all spent with them.

For dinner I find the restaurant we'd eaten at on our first night in Italy. After landing mid-morning, we'd checked into our apartment, then wandered the streets shopping and people watching. The restaurant had been a chance encounter, coming around a corner to see yellow string lights hanging off vine covered pergola jutting out into a small square far from the overpopulated tourist areas of the city. We never took out our phones to check reviews. We ate where we thought looked good, where the smells coming from the kitchen made our stomachs ache with hunger. The waitress barely spoke English and we worked through our first menu in the foreign language. Olivia knew enough from her year here in college that we were optimistic we knew what we'd ordered. Navigating a menu in Italy is generally a matter of deciding which pasta you want with which meat.

The restaurant looks the same and smells the same as I remember. I order a bottle of wine. I'm into my second glass by the time my caprese salad arrives. The tomatoes are blood red from skin to seeds and I make short work of it, realizing I haven't eaten since the coffee and croissant this morning.

"That looks amazing." The voice comes from my left and I glance over.

"It is," I say.

I'm in the corner at a small table for two. Even the tables for four are tiny, especially considering the size of the plates they bring for each course.

"Have you eaten here before?"

The question comes just as another bite enters my mouth, not realizing we were now having a conversation. I nod, politely covering my mouth with the green cloth napkin.

"It must be good, then. Do you live in Florence?"

I pick up on the Irish accent while feigning a smile while chewing. I dab the corners of my mouth with the napkin and return it to my lap, taking the moment to relish that someone thought I appeared as if I could live in this city or was perhaps just being kind in saying it.

"No, only visiting."

"Same. Well, sort of."

An attempt to return to my meal undisturbed seems fruitless. The woman is turned toward me in her chair, menu still in hand.

"Have you ordered?" I say.

"I'm waiting on the waitress to come back."

"That could be a while. If you don't order immediately you might have a long wait."

"So I've noticed."

A pause in the already light conversation. I fill it by eating the last bite of my salad. The mozzarella falls off my fork onto the table.

"Well, that has to be embarrassing," she says.

"Seems I have the table manners of a five-year-old."

I've spent three days walking the city alone, my only interaction with humans being ordering coffee or food.

"Would you like to join me? I could use the company," I say.

"How could I refuse a front row seat to this show." She moves to the chair opposite me, placing her purse that is only big enough for a credit card and a couple of euros on the table beside her.

"Where are you from?" I say.

"Kinsale, Ireland." She motions to her hair as if that was a definitive identifier of nationality. "A small town in the south. What about you?"

"I live in—Los Angeles." The lie comes before I even think about it. I don't feel like saying too much about myself, not knowing what might happen on the trip. What few coworkers I talk to at the university during summer break think I'm in Florida visiting family, a good cover for the tan from the Italian sun.

"I've always wanted to visit Los Angeles," she says. "Hollywood. The beaches. It must be so romantic."

"It is." I've never been to L.A. and change the subject. "What are you doing in Florence?"

"I'm an accountant for a global software company. Spent a couple years in Dublin and got tired of the clouds, rain, and tourists, so I looked to see what other offices were hiring."

"Good for you," I say. "Far fewer tourists in Florence."

She laughs. "At least I'm one of the tourists. I've only been here a few months, but so far it's been good," she says. "A bit lonely at times."

"I'm Avery."

"Sara, with no h." She reaches across the table with a sarcastic formal handshake that reminds me of my first interaction with Olivia. I hold her hand a moment longer than needed, frozen in flashbacks. An inadvertent flirt, and she notices, a flush of red on her cheeks.

"Are you on vacation, then?" She's chewing gum but trying to hide it. I can see the slight movement of her jaw when her mouth is closed.

I let her hand go and stutter, embarrassed from the interaction. "Oh, yeah, uh, a little work, a little fun." I can't say that I'm here to track down the man and woman who I hope have answers about how the love of my life died, then after that, I have no plans.

She smiles at the vague answer, seeming to accept it as enough. The waitress comes and Sara orders. I request my meal to wait until hers is ready, a risky move for a busy Italian kitchen.

"What do you think of Florence?" I say. Small talk has never come easy for me.

"It's beautiful, but I haven't had too much free time to explore." She looks out across the small square. Large faded letters are painted at the top of a red stone building, the word disappearing behind a wall with no hints to what it might say.

I nod. "No friends here?"

She shakes her head. "The company closes for a couple weeks for vacation, so I'm hoping to get out a bit."

"Museums, food, and wine, then?"

"Sure. Something like that." Her eyes lock with mine, a smile on her lips. "I'm hoping for something a little more fun."

"There's definitely plenty to do here."

I order a second bottle of wine, a *Brunello di Montepulciano* from a vineyard I wanted to visit on the last trip. It is dry and heavy, hitting my tongue hard. I see her wince at the first taste. She prefers white, or maybe a rose, I guess.

"Not your style?"

"I'm getting used to it. Seems that not liking red wine in Tuscany is a crime."

"What's your drink of choice?"

She glances around as if it is a state secret, then whispers across the table. "I fell in love with mojitos on a trip to Cuba a few years ago."

"That is as non-Italian as you can get."

"Right?"

"Have you found a good mojito here?"

"I have not."

Conversation continues through the meal. She makes me laugh and I realize I hadn't in a long time.

"Care for a walk?" she says.

She looks at me as she did before, as if something feral was trying to break out of a cage, then she smiles. Did her chest just heave or was she exhaling?

"I shouldn't. Busy day tomorrow," I say. Is she hitting on me?

"Shame." She says it as if there was something huge to be missed out on, experiences to be had. "Which way are you?"

I point past her. "You?"

She motions the opposite direction.

"Then I guess this is goodbye, Sara With No H."

"Such finality."

"All good things, as they say."

She has a half smile, half smirk, as she looks around for moment, then back at me.

"There's a café across the river, on *Santo Spirito*," she says. "It's mainly expats in there at night."

I nod. I know that café too well.

"Sometimes I go on Thursday nights. Half price drinks. Usually around eight o'clock. I'll be the one with the red wine, looking like I'm not sure if I like it," she says. "Come, if you like." She kisses me lightly on the cheek, and walks away.

CHAPTER THREE

I look up from my cappuccino, the only disguise I have that no one questions. I glance over at the building halfway down the long pedestrian street on the left. No movement in the windows of the apartment where the two named Pippo and Scarlet live. My only connection here. My only chance for answers. The front door remains closed. I've created a schedule in my mind. Each day the hours overlap so I'm never here the exact same time, giving me a better chance of seeing them. It sounds good in theory. If they aren't even in Florence, then it's all just a waste of time. In the evenings I visit places I know they frequented, and sometimes locations that just mean something to me and my memories of Olivia.

A first sighting is all I need, all I crave. To know they are here and not a thousand miles away, my mission over before it ever began. It will take time to build up my strength to confront him. I just need to see him first.

Pippo and Scarlet. I don't think I've said the names

aloud since I left them behind in the cloud of death that had engulfed us. Our last words had not been kind. The year has given me the distance to see them through a different lens, study them, their movements, their actions.

My final hours in Italy were a blur. A haze of confusing moments strung together that many times I've stopped to consider if they'd been real or a dream that was coming back to me from a restless night of sleep, expecting to wake and find Olivia beside me with a warm smile and warm skin. What had made sense in the rushed moments began to fall apart over the weeks and months that followed. I'd wake up and lie in bed thinking through the events in stop action, moving frame by frame until I couldn't think about it anymore, until I had to push it away to replace my thoughts with anything else.

A smile. Those red lips. Had Sara With No H been flirting with me? I had thought of it on my walk home last night then while falling asleep, the tall windows open and the night air cooling ever so slightly that my naked skin had bristled, spurred movement, excitement that I hadn't felt in so long, my hand taking control, moving autonomously from my thoughts as I did nothing to stop it.

I'm no master of seduction and far from observant at noticing signs from women, but I felt something from Sara last night that continues to pull on me, to excite me when I think about her. It could be my imagination. My body, my needs, taking over to desire something near, something real, something more than the memory of the one that died beside me in her sleep that has remained in the front of my thoughts. Maybe the year of celibacy is taking a toll on me, my adrenaline surging from the slightest attention from a pretty girl with a sexy accent wearing a plunging neckline dress, the shadows created in her cleavage from the flickering candle lingering in my thoughts.

After college ended, my best friend told me of at least four girls he knew for a fact had wanted to go out with me, and one that just wanted to fuck me. I never noticed. No clue. When asked why he didn't tell me when it was happening he just said it made it easier to get them for himself. Turns out the moans of pleasure I heard from the next room had been meant for me and I never knew it.

Four days I've been in Florence with no sign of them. Four days of sitting under a faded blue and red Cinzano umbrella outside a café staring at what seems to be an empty apartment. No lights on at night. No progress. I gave myself two weeks. Ten days left.

It strikes me they may have moved to another area of the city, or out of Florence completely. They always felt more transient than settled down. Pippo had said the apartment belonged to his family, so I choose to stick with my plan.

Or I could give up now, go enjoy myself, see the things I didn't get to see a year ago. The things I didn't see with her. But that feels wrong. Thinking of Sara also feels wrong, but she keeps finding her way back into my mind.

I spend my time trying to look as if I'm not watching for someone and contemplating what I'll actually do if I find them. What I'll say. I go through the newspaper several times even though it is all in Italian. Perhaps I'll pick up more of the language this way. It has been an ill-conceived plan from the start. My hypothesis remains unproven and I don't know if I'm smart enough to solve the theory. Or strong enough.

Answers can be dangerous. They can be enlightening, freeing, or devastating. All of the above scare me. Maybe I'm better off remaining ignorant. Leave Olivia and Italy behind, shove them into the deep corners of my brain and resist any future thoughts of them. But I know I cannot. Too much time has been spent leading up to now, to here. Too many hours of thinking about her and driving myself crazy with the need to learn more. I landed here focused, ready. My movements have been orderly and strict. Everything has gone as I planned, except for dinner with Sara. I never specifically decided not to meet anyone, make any friends. It seemed like something that didn't need to be said.

What am I even doing here if dinner with a pretty woman takes my thoughts off Olivia? Is my love for her so weak that smooth white skin from the overcast countryside of Ireland has me wanting to touch it, the first skin I've possibly longed for since Olivia's? Or am I just a typical male, testosterone fueled and turned on by a smile, an accent, and a kiss on the cheek? I of course hadn't noticed her advances or interest last night at dinner. Only in thinking back after that peck, a small stain of red remaining to be washed off my cheek at bedtime, her invitation to find her again, did I realize how oblivious I had been, that I still am.

I look to the left as a large group of Asian tourists goes past and use it as a cover to check out the apartment again. Still nothing. The two dozen people play follow the leader. The closest to the guide stay tight to her, asking questions even as she is trying to speak into the microphone that will transmit to all of the receivers with used headphones plugged into them. I can't understand or even break the language into distinct words, but do hear her say the name *Dante Alighieri*, the last name crumbling into a horrible mispronunciation.

My first girlfriend was in high school. It was short lived and easily forgotten as a whole, but she had also been my first sexual encounter. Even then I was sure it was spite sex. Her quarterback boyfriend had cheated on her. She dumped him and wanted to get even. She never said this, of course, but it was obvious. Plus, I overheard boys in the bathroom talking about us while I was hidden in the last stall between classes. In a small-town high school there are no secrets. Days play out like a version of Beverly Hills 90210 with southern accents and rusty pickup trucks.

She first seemed to notice me on a Tuesday in study hall. She had been sitting next to me for a semester and a half without knowing my name and all of a sudden was turned in her chair looking at me. Three times the assistant football coach who was forced to oversee the quiet period told her to be quiet, but never with any real implied consequences since she was one of the popular girls and from a wealthy family. By Thursday I heard we were dating, and that Saturday night I found myself in her daddy's Mustang backseat fumbling clothes off of each other for what would be two minutes of awkward enjoyment. For me.

I had turned into a damn John Mellencamp song, badly fucking a small-town redneck girl in the back of a muscle car without a rubber on. Every day I walked down the hall in my small house, past the wooden crucifix with a gaunt Tiny Jesus attached to it, the tip of his feet worn where my mother would stop each morning and evening to pray and touch that foot as if it would bring her salvation. And every day I thought that Tiny Jesus was watching me, judging me for my indiscretions against him with bare asses on black vinyl seats.

I managed to get two more weeks out of the relationship, including three more times in that cramped backseat before it ended. She never broke up with me, I just heard she was back with her old boyfriend. I didn't really care. She was pretty, but we had nothing in common and mostly I found her annoying. But she was my first, and my last for a long time.

For months I sat in church every Sunday and felt I deserved punishment such as knocking her up or at the least getting an STD from her, but neither happened. Instead I'd had sex for the first time, and several more, with a cheerleader and the class vice president. Last I heard she still lives in the same town and is divorced from the quarterback that had cheated on her way back then. I don't gloat. I live only three hours away from where I grew up and am still single.

Still no movement from the apartment and the late afternoon sun is now directly on me. I leave money on the table and leave everyone behind for a night. I need a break from Pippo and Scarlet, and even Olivia. At the shop near my place I pick up two bottles of wine and plan an evening of not remembering anything.

CHAPTER FOUR

I dream of Olivia.

People love to say things like that, that they dream of the person they love or loved, but it just isn't true. That's not how the brain works. At least you don't dream of a person in the form you know or knew them. Electric signals surge as you sleep, and your synapses might convert memories into strange manifestations of them. Your dead wife is a turtle on the side of a highway or your abusive high school boyfriend is a burning house. But to actually dream of the person, that's rare. And I did. She seemed real, felt real.

In waking hours her memory is silent, a shadow, an occasional hint of her scent on a pillow that had the power to send me into near fetal position for an hour, clutching it to my face, eyes closed, trying to imagine how she'd looked curled up on the sofa, craving to touch her, hold her, smell her.

I fear I'm forgetting her after such a short time and wonder how an old man whose wife died ten years earlier remembers the woman he was meant to spend the rest of his life with. Are the images still clear and sharp, or do they regress with time as does everything else on this earth? Granted, their time together may have lasted decades and held many more memories of love, of children and grandchildren, faces to remind him of hers in the moments he may not remember her smile as well as he once did, fireplace mantels and bookshelves covered with photographs of holidays and anniversaries and newborns. I have none of that and it wasn't until she was gone that I realized I don't even have a photograph of her, or of us together. No visual reminders left behind to ensure me that, yes, she had been real, she had been here, and she had loved me.

At the time of death, it is thought we relive our lives in an instant. Loved ones that have been lost come to welcome us, urging us to join them. If true, is this the act of a kind and giving God that wishes us to fall into afterlife gently, surrounded by warm, loving, and familiar faces? Or is it merely our brains shutting down, a lack of blood flow to its far reaches, sparking memories long forgotten, or at the least not pulled forward in many years, strobed into your conscious thoughts like the last trickle of water from a hose, or the bedroom light that fades from full brightness to dark slowly after the switch has been turned off, deprived of electricity just as the brain is of blood but refusing to be shut off quickly?

It's that darkness that scares me most. The black that comes immediately after the light. I can wake in the middle of the night and walk through my house without flipping one switch on and return to bed and fall back to sleep within moments. But for the first seconds after turning the lights out at bedtime I am frozen as I listen to every sound my house makes, that comes from outside the thin windows, that echoes inside my thoughts, and am certain I am not alone. I'm paralyzed in those moments, body pushing into the mattress as I try to hear the sounds of the house over my own breathing.

Sometimes I wake up and stare at the ceiling. My heart pounds. Sweat pours out of me. There are times I wish I wouldn't wake. That I would be lost in eternity to find her, to see my grandparents again, to not have to wonder what happens. I didn't know her long, not like the old man of my rhetoric. Our months together cannot compare to the years and lifetimes spent together by so many. I remember as a child sitting beside my grandfather after my grandmother's funeral. He was smiling and laughing, hugging people and telling them not to be sad, she was in a better place, that she wasn't suffering anymore. He was so certain of this and seemed the most content person in the room. But later, after people wearing the black suits and dresses they pulled out of the backs of closets only for these occasions left the house, I saw my grandfather alone in the kitchen. He was washing dishes, scrubbing the soapy sponge across a plate coated with sauce from a lasagna brought by a neighbor or someone from church. Once he'd cleaned the front and back, with an act of instinct, of repetition from night after night for fifty years, he held the plate over to his right to the hands that were no longer there to rinse it.

I'd seen Olivia and held her in my dream. It felt real. I heard her voice. I swear I smelled her skin, her perfume. It was a conversation we'd never had, a place we'd never been. Was it a memory that didn't have time to happen, missed from her dying too soon? The words are gone now. I don't remember what we said. They disappeared as soon as I opened my eyes. The emotion I had in the dream fades just as rapidly while the real world plays its endless game on me, sending distractions to steal the thought away; a car horn sounds from the street below, a mosquito lands on my arm and draws blood, the pressure in my bladder forces me to get out of bed.

The sun appears above the skyline, my fourth-floor apartment having better views than most. I see the top of the *duomo*, mostly blocked by a dozen buildings between here and there, but I revel in it anyway and know how much Olivia would have loved it. From my bedroom window in Kansas I have a view of six other houses and the roof of a shopping center that has a Kohl's and two Starbucks in one parking lot.

I know I should go for a jog or work on the outline for my next book that my agent has been pushing for. Instead I get in the tiny shower and run warm water with no pressure over my face and body for twenty minutes. My morning baptism as I enter the world again, wiping the sins of the day before away. Or at least the layer of salty sweat that dried on my skin overnight.

The morning after the first night she'd stayed over, I had been in the shower, the events of the evening before playing over in my mind to the point they became unreal, a fantasy. I'd turned to slide the door open, to look out and see if she was really there, asleep in my bed as she had been when I left her minutes earlier. But a shadow was approaching on the other side of the frosted glass and I froze. The door opened and she stood there, glorious in her nakedness and perfection. *Can I join you?* Yes, you can. I watched as she leaned her head back into the steaming hot water and it soaked her hair and ran down over her face and still it felt new and special. I never lost that feeling in the months I had with her. Every look at her was like it was the first time, something fresh to see, to take in and further define her. Every touch of her hand on mine, on my skin, made my heart race.

The streets are busy by the time I get to the sidewalk. Tour guides hold half open umbrellas high in the air so their large groups can find them in the crowds. The stray local walks through, weaving between tourists with ease all the while carrying on a loud and animated conversation on a cellphone. It's easy to get lost in Florence, and even easier to feel lost. The curved and winding roads seem to go nowhere until you find yourself at the archway to exit the city. You turn around to enter the labyrinth again on that perpetual hunt for the best cappuccino, the richest gelato, the quietest place to stop and kiss.

I have always felt small in this world. Inconsequential. Meaningless. I think I became a teacher to try to feel more important, that somehow I could make a difference. But mostly I sit behind a desk reading poorly written papers about Dante and F. Scott Fitzgerald and listen to college freshmen spout the same trite ideas on the symbolism in *The Grapes of Wrath* that is printed in every version of *Cliff's Notes* or written by an armchair academic on Wikipedia. Yes, please tell me your original ideas on how Ma Joad becomes stronger as Tom grows weaker.

In second grade I began to think about space and questioned everyone about how it could go on forever. How that was even possible. Teachers would say, "It just does," with the certainty of an adult not wanting to admit they didn't know. My parents would tell me it was the work of God with no further explanation, as if that is an all-encompassing answer to any question. I read books about it. Only two spacecraft have ever left our solar system, unmanned probes sending sporadic signals back through the darkness to us, and even though they are now almost 20 billion kilometers from earth, they have barely started their intergalactic road trip and won't reach the nearest star for another 40,000 years. Today I'm strolling the same streets Leonardo da Vinci once walked. He had thoughts of flying machines and robots before they were possible. Would he be impressed by what science has done or wonder why it hasn't gone further?

I stop at the café on the corner near my apartment. It is authentic enough that tourists stay out. There's no sign on an easel advertising daily specials catering to visitors, no WiFi, and the tables aren't too clean. But the cappuccino is good.

Across the square I see an old man sitting on the bench in front of a church, his loose fitting and stained lime green tank top contrasting the grey stone and thick black horizontal stripes behind him. His legs are crossed at the knees, exposing the old, sinewy muscle beneath loose skin. A gold necklace reflects light as it dangles while he hunches over with a back too tired to keep him upright anymore. He watches people as they pass, his eyes sometimes stopping and focusing much farther out. I wonder if he is thinking of someone he lost, his childhood love who spent her life beside him, raising children and keeping them all fed before passing quietly in their bed, when a woman walks up and sits beside him. He turns with a smile and they kiss the kiss of a much younger couple, his arm then goes around her and together they watch the tourists walk by. This is their day, I think. Watching the world revolve, together, and it is beautiful.

My grandfather had frozen for a moment with that soapy plate hovering in midair. When his body remembered, he twitched and looked lost for a moment, then he turned on the cold water and rinsed the soap off the white and burgundy china.

CHAPTER FIVE

There's no breeze today. It's a smothering heat as I walk through the narrow streets. My shirt is matted to skin, soaked through with sweat. It will be a good day to sit and drink something cold in the shade. Outside is still better than inside my apartment with no air conditioning.

I brought no shorts with me, only khakis and other lightweight slacks after seeing how the locals dressed last time. I come far short of blending in with them, but also don't look like the majority of tourists. It's the camouflage I need. The cover to fade into the background and not be noticed.

I walk past the boutiques as beautiful people walk out carrying large white bags with names printed on them in small, clean letters. Most of the names mean nothing to me. I don't pay attention to fashion. My wardrobe is from the large anchor stores at the mall. When I find a shirt or pair of pants I like, I buy them in each color they have and I'm good for another year. Maybe two.

Money isn't a concern. I live within my means. I make enough off my teaching to live comfortably. The earnings from my books go directly into savings and investment accounts. With each new release there's a surge in income. I'm fortunate to have a series of books that kids look for and libraries stock as soon as a new one comes out. I was once approached about licensing the titles for an animated series, but so far nothing has come from that. I'm happy to be successful yet still retain a level of anonymity other than my occasional book readings.

As I planned my return to Italy, I dipped into savings more than usual. Generally I only do when I need a new laptop, when I bought my car, or paying for the trip with Olivia a year ago. The things that put a strain on the salary of a college professor. The time I spent here before spoiled me. I lived beyond my means and experienced things I didn't think possible. I can't replicate that, but decided I didn't have to stick to a budget, either.

The blast of cold air sends a shiver through me as I enter the Deutsche Bank branch a block off of *Piazza Della Repubblica*, around the corner from the Hard Rock café that feeds more American tourists daily than all of the small homestyle restaurants in the city combined.

"Buongiorno, Signor Chase. Hello!" The man is wearing a suit more expensive than the one I bought yesterday and a large Panerai watch on his wrist that constantly finds its way to show beneath the end of his shirt sleeve, the cobalt blue face grabbing attention as he motions me to a desk to be assisted. Eugenio was merely the greeter.

I have been in Florence only a few days and it is my second time in for a cash withdrawal, my name remembered for that special level of customer service demanded by people with much more money than myself.

When I returned home a year ago I was destroyed by what happened to Olivia. Weeks were spent in darkened rooms with wine and food being delivered directly to the house. The school year was nearing and I had been in danger of not being mentally ready to stand in front of a hundred disinterested freshmen.

A phone call one night to order delivery and the awkward teen on the other end said my credit card had been rejected. I tried another with the same result.

After a night of Chinese leftovers from the fridge, I surfaced to find my bank accounts frozen, drained, and damaged. My local bank branch was mystified and further investigation showed that not only was my personal checking and savings hit, but one of my investment accounts had been depleted. All in, the damage was more than $230,000 gone. Police were involved and hearing of my overseas trip they determined my credit cards had been compromised at a café, store, or a tech savvy thief with an RFID reader walking through the packed tourist crowds. It took nearly half a year, but bank insurance recouped some of the money for me and I quickly moved to put my funds into more secure facilities.

"Two thousand, please."

No second looks at the amount as quiet keys are tapped on the computer. Minutes later a young lady with an envelope appears. It is handed to the man at the desk and then to me, the hierarchy of the system. It is not recounted or double checked and never is the money actually visible. I place it in the inside breast pocket of my sports coat and shake hands.

When walking around Florence you see the class structures at work, even more than in New York or Chicago. Not even considering the standard grade of tourists who are dressed as if they are headed to Six Flags for the day, you have the wide gamut of locals.

The delivery men and laborers, sweaty and dirty and in constant motion even in the heat are juxtaposed by the men in $5,000 suits made from fabric so shiny that they could reflect sunlight, walking with women in dresses straight off the catwalk, feet in heels that somehow levitate above the cracked stone sidewalks and roads that trip up mere mortals who dare to take their attention off their steps and glance at their phone, only to trip and fall face first to the street.

I came more prepared this time. Only cash. I'd driven to Chicago to set up the account and moved more than enough money to cover expenses on the trip. The only credit card I brought for emergencies is locked in the safe in my rental apartment.

The sweat that had cooled and dried on my skin inside the cold building turned to liquid again moments after stepping back outside. I pass the Hard Rock and the line waiting to get in.

CHAPTER SIX

A cab drops me off on *Santo Spirito* at a quarter after eight. I feel eager and ambivalent at the same time, and walk the opposite direction of the café to kill a few minutes. I'm nervous to see Sara again and still hesitant to do so. For every part of it that feels wrong, another part feels right. It has been a year and Olivia is dead. I try to convince myself I have the right to have fun. To be happy. Even if only for a few hours.

Seeing the street, the plain wooden door with peeling paint, it comes back to me. This is where it started. Somehow I forgot about it, blocked it out, pushed it away.

We'd come here. I don't know how Olivia had known about it. It was a Thursday night like tonight, I think. Not that the day matters. They all blur into each other on a trip like that. Weekdays are indiscernible from weekends and the nights go on forever when you are with someone you love in another land. Time is told only in days and you regret the moment you stop and count, realizing you have fewer days left on the trip than those that have passed. You want it to go on forever. The food is better on vacation, the sex is better, the air around you feels more alive. And two weeks goes by in the blink of an eye.

It's a residential neighborhood. A few *tabacchi* shops and cafés, but mostly apartments. In a country where air conditioning is not the norm people stay outside whenever they can, and it is no different in Florence. Children are playing soccer on the street when no cars are coming. Their families sit on the steps, smoking and all talking at the same time. It is loud and busy compared to my suburban Kansas City life. In the small dose so far, I enjoy it. I know I would tire of it after time. I would want wide open spaces and silence. I don't do well with chaos and noise. I crave simplicity.

Every summer day was spent outside as a child, even in the rain. I would leave first thing and not return home until after sunset. In that small rural town in the center of the country that was safe. Or felt safe. It was before 24-hour news cycles put fear into people. Before September 11. Before two dozen channels showing true crime shows. It wasn't even a matter of parents trusting their children or other people. It's just how it was.

I glance at my watch. 8:30. I cross the street and head back the other direction. A few minutes later I'm standing outside the café. The front is the same drab stone color as the rest of the buildings around it. The one window is covered on the inside with a thick drape. Only the noise filtering through the heavy door and a small sign give any indication that there is a business behind it. I remember the worn wood frame with cracked paint and how it had felt against my fingers when I'd arrived with Olivia. I had touched it as we entered, a need for a physical connection, a sensation to distract me from the sensory overload I was expecting inside the café, something to center my thoughts on, a tactile white noise.

I step inside the café and a shock wave hits my body, temporarily rendering me paralyzed as my head swims in a feeling of *deja vu*. It has only been a year, so of course nothing changed. Nothing changes in Italy. The smells and sounds were identical to when Olivia and I had walked through the door together. I recall thinking then that it felt like stepping into a musty theater, a foreign language film with no subtitles playing, the volume turned up too loud on old speakers, causing you to wince at the sound until finally you grow used to it.

Olivia had turned to me then, already elated at the sensation, grabbed my arm, and pulled me into the middle of everything I hate. Noises and smells and loud people yelling to be heard over all the other voices. Stale cigarette smoke and the malodor from years of sweaty people congregating in a small space with inadequate ventilation.

"Isn't this great?" Olivia said.

I'd given a smile to show my approval while trying to avoid rubbing up against people as she'd pulled me through the crowd, her hand holding my arm the only thing that kept me from running away. But it was for her and I would have done anything for her. I did do anything for her.

It is just as loud tonight and the rankness of the air is the same, but I recover from the moment of incapacitation and work my way into the congregation of young and energetic expatriates. The common language appears to be English of varying accents, though I hear some speaking French and German. I'm almost to the back wall, which wouldn't seem a difficult accomplishment based on the size of the café, but navigating the tightly packed bodies proves monumental.

I finally see her. She is sitting alone at a table for two, a glass of wine in her hand, a smile on her lips. She is a witness to the crowd, a voyeur, sitting on the edge of the madness and watching. There is nothing judgmental in her gaze as she takes in the party around her. Perhaps a hint of jealousy. Her eyes meet mine as I emerge and I see that same smile, that same light in her eyes from before.

My mind runs through what I should say but I keep having to push aside the film noir clichés.

Come here often?

What's a girl like you doing in a place like this?

She stands as I reach the table and leans in. I misunderstand and move to hug her, turning my face at the wrong moment so that her lips land on mine rather than my cheek in the attempted European greeting. My embarrassment is washed away with her honest laughter and her smile.

We separate and I look down into her green eyes, knowing I have a schoolboy grin on my face, the same I would have had the first time I ever kissed a girl when I was sixteen in a baby blue Mustang.

"So, have you missed me?" she says. The Irish lilt has a gravitational pull, wanting me to hear more.

"I did."

It is partly true. Olivia is always on my mind, but since dinner two nights ago my brain has gone back and forth between memories of one woman and growing desires to touch another. To touch Sara With No H. I had trouble getting to sleep with feelings of guilt in being attracted to someone else. Her voice was in my head.

"How was work today?" I say.

"Do you really want to know?"

"I do."

"It was fine. Paying invoices and transferring funds to our corporate offices in California," she says. "Very exciting stuff."

She talks and I keep reminding myself to pay attention as I get distracted looking at her smooth skin, getting lost in her voice. It's been a year since I last touched a woman and here before me sits a beautiful young lady somehow interested in my company.

"What do you do back in Los Angeles?"

Lies get difficult to track. By putting in truths, especially boring ones, the deceit is more manageable, seems less severe and easier to recover from in the chance I ever come clean.

"I teach literature at a small state university." An ambiguous answer. I could make up the name of a school. She wouldn't know just as I wouldn't if she were to do the same for a location in Ireland.

"You're a professor?" Her smile is intoxicating and a bit mischievous. I consider a Nabokov reference but hold it back.

Her manner and voice relax me. She is comfortable to be with, to talk to. I want to extend our evening as long as possible and it's only begun.

"Do you—" A laugh floats over the crowd, impeding my thoughts, cutting through the dissonance of voices. My body reacts, muscles tighten, skin vibrates with the sound as if fingernails were pulled down a chalkboard.

I force a smile, a reflex, a facade, hoping it matches whatever Sara is saying. I cannot hear her. I can only hear behind me. The laugh has turned to talking, still above the noise, demanding the attention of anyone in its gravitational pull. My stomach turns.

I know that voice but can't turn to look. My eyes stay on Sara, deep into a story about her childhood in rural Ireland or a wild college party. I don't know. Her sound is gone, stolen into the ether by another that binds itself to my subconscious, bringing only memories to the foreground.

I heard that voice for the first time in this same café. Olivia and I were sitting at a table not far from the one I share now with Sara. We were discussing what to do the next day. I seem to recall we were considering going to the *Gallerie dell'Accademia* to see the artwork inside, ending with the magnificent original statue of David, or staying in our rental apartment and making love all day. We were presenting arguments to defend our choices.

The voice was then as it is now, a wavelength all its own, coming through the static clearly. It was loud and obnoxious, presiding over the room whether it was deserved or not. Olivia had laughed at his jokes from afar, though they were simple and more than a bit rude. The grown-up version of playground humor.

Eventually we'd seen the owner of the voice and he matched it perfectly. Six-foot-two, slender, and somewhere in his mid-30's, I guessed. He wore white pants with a light green silk shirt unbuttoned to the base of his sternum. Hair was swooped over in a perfect arc that would make David Beckham in his prime envious. A tightly trimmed and narrow beard outlined his jaw and a matching mustache touched the rim of his upper lip, leaving a channel of skin below his nose. He wasn't unattractive. I'm sure most would consider him handsome. I found him unpleasant.

Attached to his side was a woman probably a few years younger and beautiful in the girl-next-door meets exotic dancer way. She had long naturally straight hair that defied her brown skin. A white camisole shirt clung to her; the V-neck cut formed arcs over perfect breasts. Her smile was vibrant, and she laughed when he did and listened when he talked, staring at him as if he were the center of attention he craved to be. I could tell there was more to the liaison. His eyes would constantly meet hers for approval, support. He relied on this consent as equals in the performance, he the showman, her the producer, the critic.

People had to listen. They had no choice. He dominated the space, taking over the conversation with his own pedestrian anecdotes and improper jokes. He would be a #metoo movement and Human Resources nightmare in the real world. But in a dirty expat café in Florence, he was the life of the party, an English speaking, Italian accented boor that no one ever had the balls to tell he wasn't that entertaining as long as it meant they could be loud, drunk, and obnoxious right along with him.

Olivia was enthralled to the point that our own conversation was left hanging with no resolution to the urgent matter of naked paintings or naked us. I gave up trying to light that spark again and reluctantly listened to the new master of ceremony along with the rest of the café.

I have been standing in shadows on hot days watching their door, looking for them, walking past restaurants and cafés we'd gone to, nothing. Then here, now. While I'm with her.

"Avery?"

They had taken over our night from afar last year, never allowing me to recover and bring Olivia's eyes back to mine in sweet romantic banter.

"Are ya there?" A hand touches my arm. I jump.

"What?"

"Where were you?" Sara says. "Are ya okay?"

I'm not sure I am. I want to turn and see him. He is after all the reason I'm back in Italy. I hadn't expected to lay eyes on him until I got to Positano, but maybe that's just where I wanted to find him, back where it happened, where my Olivia died. I couldn't be sure I'd ever find him, but here he is behind me.

"I'm fine," I say. "I'm sorry. I got distracted."

She glances past me at the mob that moves and acts as one creature, the loud voice from the center acting as its heartbeat, keeping the beast alive. It's a symbiotic relationship. He needs the crowd so he can feel important, and the audience requires him to entertain them, to give validation to their excessive drinking and celebration with nothing real to celebrate. With either gone, silence would fall across the room and break into a dozen different quiet conversations, each more mundane than the last. Someone would try to take over, to fill the void, but it would fail.

Sara goes silent in the awkwardness of the moment. I want to give her my full attention, but I can't. I may as well be alone, and likely will be soon.

I finally raise the courage to turn. He is hidden, blocked by moving heads and arms raised in the air, drink glasses aloft for no reason. But the voice is constant, a homing beacon to center my gaze upon. One person moves left, another right, and there he is. The same white pants as a year ago but this time a blue shirt and plenty of chest. I see his smile I know too well from so many nights of drinking and reveling in nothing but the fact that we were there and alive and able to do so. His head turns, eyes taking in the adoring fans waiting for his next joke or vulgarity. I swear his eyes meet mine for the shortest amount of time, but nothing in his tell me he recognizes me. I turn back around to face Sara.

"You want to go somewhere else?" Sara says. Her hands reach across the table and hold mine, fingers stroke my skin with a soft, caring touch that seems to imply there is more to be had.

CHAPTER SEVEN

He is still present in my mind even as I watch Sara move around my apartment. I have gone against my own orders, my reason for being here, but her subtlety steals my attention, captures my imagination, and slowly takes my thoughts off Pippo and Scarlet. Her hands intentionally move across surfaces as she looks at the few pieces of art and knick-knacks around the rental intended to make it feel more Italian. She stops in front of the window, the sheer curtains open as always, and I see her shoulders drop as she takes in the view of the *duomo* lit up at night, the red tiles glowing.

"How gorgeous," she says. Everything sounds better with her accent.

I sit on the small European sized sofa that would barely be a love seat at home, my arm stretched across the back as I watch her. I cleaned up before leaving and had a bottle of wine with two glasses set out in a rare moment of confidence. I never really thought she would be here with me.

"Were you planning on this?" she says. "On me coming back here with ya?"

I smile. She pours two glasses and hands me one over my shoulder then moves around the end of the sofa as if floating. One leg bends and goes under her as she sits down beside me, angled toward me, looking at me.

"What happened back there?" she says.

A head shake, a sip, a pause to think, to delay.

"Nothing. Just a little panic attack, maybe." That's where I am, that I would rather say I had a panic attack than tell her the truth. "It was too noisy, too smoky."

She nods. Her eyes are taking me in, moving from feature to feature and I feel vulnerable, open. My pulse races and my confidence fades, replaced by the awkward pubescent version of myself. But she doesn't seem to notice, the bare skin of her knee where her dress pulled up when she sat rests on top of my leg. I feel movement, excitement growing, and shift my position in an attempt to hide it.

"Did you know that man?" she says. "The loud one."

I consider telling her I do, that I'd spent more than two weeks with him, his beautiful companion, and my now dead girlfriend. That he is why I am here. It will feel good. With Sara I think it would be easy. She's merely a character passing through my story. A distraction. There's a sense of safety in her. Without names it would be impossible to retell with certainty, nothing to identify the guilty or incriminate the innocent. I've wanted to tell someone for so long. These stories have been mine alone and too many hours have been spent reliving them in dark rooms, trying to find what I'd missed then, notes made in longhand on legal sized paper to keep the memories from disappearing, to see the details that are blurred in memories. A version of the truth comes out, unplanned, not thought through well enough to be presented publicly. I would be destroyed in cross examination.

"I was in Florence before," I say. "With my girlfriend."

She pulls back so subtly that it is almost imperceptible. It's the slightest change in posture, in her breathing.

"Really? When?"

"A year ago." I need an outline. Preparation like for one of my books, broad strokes speckled with details in front of me to know where I am going. "She's not— "

I don't know if I've ever said it. There's no one I would have told or even could have. It had become a secret the moment it happened. As soon as I left Florence that morning I was forced to push it to the back, attempt to erase half a year of my life, or at least the last two weeks.

"She died."

Sara's hand grabs mine and squeezes. She searches my face, perhaps looking for the truth, a human lie detector sensing my honesty, not landing on my eyes until I squeeze back. In a glance I know she believes me in one of the few truths I've told her.

"It's okay," I say. "We'd been to that bar. I guess it was just too much being back."

"I'm so sorry. You shoulda told me. We could have gone somewhere else. Anywhere else."

"It's fine. It's why I'm here. To face my demons, you could say. To put her behind me."

The silence isn't awkward or uncomfortable, just present. She is looking at me with a question not far beneath the surface, wanting to come out. The air in the room is still.

"I didn't mean to— "

"No, no. Thank you for telling me," she says. "Do you want me to leave?"

"No." I shake my head and grab her hands. "I want you to stay."

A year of thinking only of Olivia, pining for her, dreaming of her. I have changed my look, my physique, through months of harmful habits then working hard to make myself better, all to come back here to find out what happened. Answers, closure, revenge, whatever you want to call it. The moment ahead of me had not been considered or imagined possible. But as it approaches, I see its importance, its role in my recovery.

She leans into my body and kisses me. Her neck stretches for her lips to meet mine. I reach behind her and place my hand flat on the bare skin above her low-cut dress back. I feel an energy from her, a pulsation at my touch, an invitation to take more. Thoughts of Pippo and Scarlet are gone, pushed aside enough to enjoy this moment, this woman. Olivia is still with me, though. She always is.

Once again, I'm that boy in the back seat of a Mustang, hands exploring and fumbling. Lips wanting more. I stand and pull her up with me and wrap my arms around her, now able to kiss her well, strong, leaning down into her. I feel her body, her neck, stretch for my lips. Tongues meet. She has unbuttoned my shirt without my feeling it and her hand is on my bare chest.

Sara steps back and pulls the thin dress strap over her shoulder and lets it drop to her arm and reaches for the other one. I stop her, my hand rests on top of hers.

"What's wrong?" she says.

"Let me."

CHAPTER EIGHT

Soft light from an overcast sky filters in through the open floor to ceiling windows as sheer white curtains flap dramatically in the breeze like it's the set for a Merchant Ivory film. Sara is beside me, still sleeping. Her naked back is smooth and glows as if a master of chiaroscuro painted her, a Rubenesque figure of skin and pores rather than oils on wood. It is a moment to live in, to go back to on future days to relive and remember once I am alone again. A memory to replace a memory.

I stroke her skin, fingertips barely making contact, up her back, across her shoulders. She stirs with a soft exhale and rolls, giving my hand free passage to her full breasts. I lean over to kiss her and as I do, her hand moves down to touch me. My muscles tense at the sensation. Her eyes meet mine when she finds me ready.

We make love again in the long morning light until we sweat from the friction of skin against skin and from the Tuscan sun outside heating the air around us in the apartment with no air conditioning. It is better than last night and I can tell we both know that, feel that. The first-time sex fumbling and kissing was gone. Without the alcohol, the distraction at the bar, we wake up naked and comfortable with each other. We've now seen each other walk nude across the room to bring us more wine, to go to the bathroom. No embarrassment. No shame. Exposed. Free. Excited.

After, we lay there, still entwined, sweaty and catching our breath, holding each other. Her hand stays on me, touching me in a way that says she wants to, that she enjoys feeling me even when expended. I think about leading her to the shower to wash her, explore her more, then remember the tiny stall with a folding frosted glass door that is difficult enough for one to maneuver.

She is my first since Olivia. I wondered over the past year if it would be difficult once the opportunity arose. It wasn't. I still love Olivia, but also know she is gone. I'm not cheating on a girlfriend or recovering from a breakup that I hope will end up in us getting back together. It's just sex. A one-night stand. Or two nights, if I'm lucky.

"You're leaving soon." Her voice is soft. Her finger traces patterns on my chest, messages that I cannot decipher.

I feel the urge to tell her everything, the rest of the truth. To ask her to join me in Positano, at least until her vacation is over. But it has only been one night, followed by one morning, and I choose to not act impulsively.

"Why do you say that?"

"Your suitcase is packed."

I look over at the dresser, my suitcase open on top, clothes folded neatly inside. She doesn't know that I never unpack. Each roadside hotel I stay in on my book tours blends in with the last when driving around the Midwest, reading to children in the morning and looking for the best meal each town has that night. I'm an expert on the greatest and worst steak houses in six states. I don't unpack because I want to leave quickly the next morning. They aren't luxury hotels with views of the ocean, just cloned rooms with small red bibles in the dresser drawer and stale pancakes at the free breakfast.

"I have at least one more day."

I had planned on leaving after picking up my suit this morning. I know there is a train just past noon that will take me to Rome, then connect for the ride to Naples. From there it is the dirty *Circumvesuviana* commuter train that makes the "L" in Chicago look clean and modern. But *he* is here, I know that now. There is no rush to go. I will take it a day at a time, though.

"Does one more day mean one more night as well?" she says.

"It does."

"Could that night include me?"

"I would like that."

I'll soak in the attention and affection as long as I can. Perhaps after I am done I can find her again, but I know that this is a Florence fling, nothing real to survive outside the romanticism of this city. This isn't love and cannot turn into it. The lies I've already told her would eliminate any chance of that. For now, I will make love with her until I have to leave.

Besides, without knowing what will happen when I finally confront Pippo, I may be leaving the city quickly for the second time, eager to get back across the sea, to the perceived safety and relative obscurity of my home that looks like the one across from it and the ones on either side except for the color of the shutters. I never feared Pippo when I was last here. He was annoying but gracious, complicated in a simple way. His moods changed quickly but were easy to see and adjust for, to accommodate. Now, I'm not so sure. The memories I've replayed over and over begin to tell a different story of him, a story I either missed then or am fabricating now.

"Where are you going next?"

I consider my answer. Too much information can be a bad thing, but I already feel guilty for lying about where I'm from and why I'm here.

"South," I say. "To Positano."

I feel her take a deep breath. It's a standard reaction to thinking about the Amalfi Coast. When all you know is the photographs, you can't help but want to be there. The scenery evokes relaxation, romanticism, and sex. Once you've been, you know it's that rare place that lives up to expectations, if not exceeds them. The water really is that blue and the people really are that beautiful. The food tastes better and the liquor gets you drunk faster. There are still the crowds of tourists boating in from Sorrento and Naples during the day, but find the narrower lanes in Positano as the sun dips toward the horizon and the last ferry has left for the day, climb to the top of the hill in Amalfi, and there are moments you are alone with the warm air around you and the water below. I want to see Sara there, to walk those beaches and streets with her after just one night. It's a shift from a year of only thinking of Olivia and those beaches and streets. A murmur in my heart, an ache deep inside, a guilt for thinking of someone else, for being with someone else. I try to push it away. I want this moment. I need it. I need to feel normal and wanted if only for a short time.

"Can we start our last night together early?" she says.

"I'd like that."

We move between cuddling, napping, and kissing easily, hands roaming and touching, exciting each other and making us feel good, until she is out of bed, her dress covering her luscious skin. She leaves reluctantly, seeming to want to stay as much as I want her to. But it will be only a few hours and I'll see her again. I'll allow myself to fall further into her distraction, her warmth, her sweetness. It is a break I didn't expect but feel I deserve, that I tell myself I deserve, after a year of pining and sitting in darkened rooms in the middle of the day. She is a gift when I need it most.

A long, lingering kiss at my open front door in the fourth floor walk up. My hand moves to her breast outside her floral print dress as a woman from the next apartment comes out into the hallway, shaking her head at us as she locks her door and continues her disapproval while walking down the stairs.

I shower and let the warm water run over me, refreshing me, waking me from the dream so I can enter the real world again. Once I do, I am renewed. My time back has been spent burdened by the past, the ballast of flashbacks at every familiar corner, obstructing me from any enjoyment of the beautiful surroundings. My thoughts are freer this morning. My steps lighter. I catch myself smiling when I glance in a shop window. I get the cappuccino my body craves, having gotten used to the caffeine boost every morning. At home I rarely drink coffee. It puts me on edge.

It is two cities, two unique personalities, day and night in Florence. I enjoy them both. The life is on the streets during the day. Shopping and eating, couples walk with bodies close, their arms brushing each other on each swing. It's too hot to touch much more with the sun beating down on the unforgiving stones that reflect the heat up at you, hitting you from two directions at once, touch replaced with smiling glances and laughter. There's a change when the light fades. Hands go around shoulders and bodies, pulling each other closer. The life moves indoors, to the restaurants and cafés and bedrooms. The pace slows. Conversations last longer. Dinner takes three hours with no waiters constantly checking on you or leaving the bill. *When you're ready,* as they say back home, in a hurry to clear the table for the next group in order to earn another tip, and another after that.

The tailor is opening his shop as I arrive, thirty minutes after the sign says he would be there. Italian time is fluid. Watches are worn for style, not function. Clocks exist to give a general idea, not exactness. Make dinner plans and it is assumed you will show up sometime in the evening. Even the trains and ferries are reluctant to follow a schedule.

After a last fitting to make sure everything is correct, I decide to wear the suit out. He adjusts my hat, lowering the brim closer to my brow, and I leave. It isn't far to my apartment so I drop off my old clothes and continue to walk the city, taking my time before meeting with Sara.

I stop at a bookstore to browse the shelves and consider picking up a favorite novel translated into Italian, a Steinbeck perhaps, maybe Hemingway, then stop kidding myself and look at Stephen King books. I love the texts I teach but my tastes for enjoyment are much more pedestrian. I'm disappointed when I find that *IT* in Italian is still *IT*. As I pass the children's section, I scan the shelves out of curiosity and find several of my kid's mysteries in Italian. *Bambini Sul Caso*. It's a strange feeling, seeing your name on a book, even if it is a pseudonym, with a title in a different language.

My secret identity remains so with Sara. She knows only my first name. Come to think of it, I only know hers. The irony, if she were hiding from something as well. We know little of each other so far and perhaps none of it is true. I pause as I think of meeting her where I first ate with Olivia in Florence, then how we met at the same club where Pippo and Scarlet first entered my life. A coincidence, I'm sure.

I planned on writing great novels. Sweeping, deep stories that cross generations and offer the reader every emotion as they connect with the characters. Subtle symbolism and story arcs that come together beautifully. I tried. The stories never came. I have more first pages written than I care to admit, all filed away in a folder on my computer, destined to never be seen again. If ever I succeed and produce a novel a publisher deems worthy and accolades roll in, I will go to that folder and delete all my old writing to make sure it doesn't get out into the world accidentally, tarnishing my reputation. But for now, all I can write are children's books.

It was an afternoon in my neighborhood library that changed my course. A local author was reading to a group of children not far from where I sat with my laptop open, the cliché blank screen taunting me. I kept hearing the author read. She was probably mid-50's and telling a story I'm sure she meant to be entertaining and educational, a teaching moment about friendship. As she read I was editing her in my mind, crossing out words and adding new ones. Before I realized it, I was typing my edits. When she finished the book, the children sat there. A few parents clapped, trying to get a reaction from their kids, but it was paltry and forced at best. I checked the calendar just inside the front door of the library and wrote down every reading scheduled for the month in the children's section, and I was there for all of them. I learned more from hearing what they were doing wrong than I had from years in college creative writing classes. I figured if I can't tell my story simply and succinctly enough for children, I can never tell it for grown-ups. Shortly after that, I started my first *Kids on the Case* book. It was out of spite more than ambition. If they can do this, I can do it better. An agent agreed and eight months later I had a publisher and my first release date scheduled.

I don't know if it was intentional, but wandering takes me on a wide route through the city, eventually to the end of the street where Pippo and Scarlet live, to the café I've been sitting outside of daily. The thought of them brings me back to reality, his stink to my mind. I don't risk walking past the entry to the apartment. I don't know what I expect to see. Do I think they'll be standing outside, talking and laughing? *Remember when that American girl died in our guest room? Good times.*

CHAPTER NINE

Olivia and I stayed up late almost every night when we were home. The television would play in the background while we sat and talked, laughed, kissed. I spent my morning lectures tired, but the bleary-eyed freshman didn't notice through their own hangovers and exhaustion from being free of their parents and curfews.

I always woke before her, used to early hours for my morning classes. I didn't even own an alarm clock and would use my phone for the rare days I knew I had to be up earlier than usual. I enjoyed that pleasure of seeing her first; sleeping, comfortable, grinning, sometimes drooling, and always beautiful. When her eyes would finally flutter open I'd squeeze mine shut quickly and dramatically. Her finger would poke into my chest, just at the edge of being too hard.

"I know you're awake."

I pretended she woke me, stretching my arms and looking around the room as if I had never seen it until

I was looking at her. *Oh, hey, what are you doing here?* It never got old to me and she pretended it never did for her.

We rarely had plans for the weekends. Everything was spontaneous. If I ever suggested something early in the week she would always answer, "We'll see." She liked to be home, which worked for me. At times I wanted to show her off, go out and be seen with her, but would push that selfishness away to cuddle with her on my living room floor. It was comfortable. It was romantic.

I get the occasional publisher requested road trips for book readings, the never-ending marketing to children and their parents to get another sale and promote the next book. My contract requires it, as much as I dislike the events. I've never enjoyed flying and my agent works to keep the schedule within driving distance of my home when she can. The long hours on the road were altered when Olivia started going with me. A quick in-and-out of a city was turned into an adventure. I found myself enjoying days and nights in exotic locations such as Tulsa, St. Louis, and Little Rock.

We were in Dallas for a long weekend and two scheduled events at different book stores. We enjoyed eating big Texas meals and seeing big Texas hair and taking in several of the city's museums. The 25th floor room of the Hyatt overlooking downtown provided a backdrop for sleepless nights filled with enjoying each other, naked bodies on display high above for anyone who could see that far.

"Why do you like me?" Her voice blended with the

darkness of the hotel room, the only light coming from the city skyline outside the wide windows.

"What do you mean?"

"You know, why do you like me? What is it about me?" She paused. "Why me?"

The question was pointed in the wrong direction. If anyone should wonder "why me," it was her about me. She came into my life unexpectedly and like a freight train, taking my emotions by storm. I didn't look back once and wonder why, I just tried to enjoy every moment and every kiss.

"Your smile," I said.

"That's it? My smile? Nothing else?"

I acted as if I was pondering the question, considering what else drew me to her, looking her up and down as I did.

"Your laugh is sweet, too."

I felt her turn to look at me while we are curled up in the king-sized bed, barely covered with the last remaining sheet that hadn't been pushed off in moments of passion.

"But if pressed, I guess I'd have to say your boobs."

She laughed but was in a weird position and it came out as a snort, which made her laugh harder and snort harder, causing me to start laughing.

"Definitely your boobs."

That's what it was like with Olivia. She was always fun, always sweet.

She was quiet in the seat beside me on the drive home, legs pulled up underneath her, leaning on the armrest.

We left late at night at the end of that weekend after one last big dinner before heading out. It was a couple hours into the drive. There were spots of light in the distance where houses sat miles apart from each other surrounded by farmland. The stereo was on low. Alexi Murdoch's Scottish accent tilted lyrics ran through the air around us.

This was what I'd been missing without knowing it. The quiet moments, together but alone in thoughts. It was more than relaxing.

Her hand came to my shoulder so softly I almost didn't feel it. I reached up and placed mine on top of it, stroking her skin with my fingertips.

"Can you pull over?"

I glanced at her and back at the road, the rear-view mirrors. No headlights for miles on the desolate highway. The side of the road was wider than the travel lane and I pulled all the way over until my right tires were just off onto the dried earth.

"Everything okay?"

She rested her head on my arm and I kissed the top of her head, then she turned to accept my lips on hers, long and slow. Her hand moved from my shoulder and down my chest until it landed on my thigh. We didn't say anything, just letting the music continue in the glow of orange dash lights of the German automobile with seats reclined. Twice the car shook from large trucks flying past at over 80 miles per hour, my mind momentarily pulled from my lips on her breasts with her body over mine to wondering if the drivers knew what was happening in the parked car with headlights off in the middle of nowhere. It was soft but intense, more than just sex. Lips on lips and eyes looking into eyes. I watched her as she finished, her hands on either side of my face, her body trembling in a release of emotion.

After, we stayed connected for a long time, her bare chest against mine. I thought I sensed a sadness in her exhales, but it was probably just the vast darkness outside the windows. Oklahoma surrounded us in the night, low clouds blocking the stars that should have been plentiful in the wide-open space.

We were back on the road, cruise control set at ten over the speed limit, and still no words spoken, just a comfort between us. I reached over and stroked her thigh with my hand and she was asleep.

We did things I never imagined in my wildest high school fantasies when the most you know about sex is the basic instructions. Part A goes into Part B. Repeat. At sixteen you don't think about love or romance or creating pleasure for your partner, just getting off. What was eight minutes all in the first time, including getting undressed and dressed again in a cramped back seat, becomes hours when you are older. It's not about getting there fastest but exploring and savoring. Tasting and holding. Giggling and getting sweaty.

I learned so much from Olivia, but always in the gentlest ways. A hand moved slightly, a pace sped up or slowed down. The look in her eyes when something was just right.

CHAPTER TEN

The *Gallerie dell'Accademia* is understated from the outside. It doesn't crave attention like the Louvre with its glass pyramid or the Guggenheim's spiraling architecture. It blends in with all the other buildings around it, standing out only from the long line of visitors at the front door most of the day.

Olivia and I had gone on the third day of our trip. Our trial from the night before at the café had been settled out of court, with half the day spent naked in bed, the other half at the *Accademia.* It was a fair outcome, enjoyed by both, twice for her.

We moved slowly, trying not to miss anything. The trip to Italy was for her, for this. She told me about her favorite paintings, pointing out details I would never notice on my own, deepening my appreciation for what went into making the art. At least in that moment I appreciated it. The cold and lifeless statues I had never cared for were brought to life with her descriptions of blocks of marble being excavated from a quarry not far to the north in Carrera, the tons of stone being carried to an artist's studio to be chiseled and worked into what they would become. It left me thinking about the stone that had been buried for millions of years that now attracted people to come stare at them, marvel at them.

We were halfway through the museum that day when a laugh shattered the unwritten rule of silence in the halls. Perhaps it is written. I had never experienced someone being so loud in a museum, therefore wasn't sure on the regulations. I glanced at her and we both knew who it was. A second laugh then the voice that followed confirmed it. She smiled, I didn't.

The night before had ended when the couple finally left the café, loud invitations to move on to somewhere livelier and with better wine were cheered, but in the end only a few people followed them out the door into the darkness. The café got quiet for a while then started to empty, the revelers drained and ready for rest. We left a short time later, walking to the Arno for a late view of the river at night, when you can't see how brown the water is, before going back to our apartment.

They were behind us in the museum but gaining quickly, as their time spent in front of each piece of art was limited to moments, if they even paused at all. I drew Olivia to a painting that I found not too interesting, asking her to tell me about it, only to kill time while the man and woman worked their way past us. Voices got louder and heads turned to see the disruption, the pair never noticed anyone who didn't appreciate their running dialogue about the art, the building, and occasional swipes at how some tourists were dressed. At one point he switched to Italian and the only word I caught was Walmart in his elaborate joke, which was followed by more laughter from him and his beautiful companion.

We could still hear them, but they were past us, so I lost interest in the painting and we moved on. It had been a fair plan but flawed as most conceived quickly are. When we arrived in the Tribunal room, custom built to house the towering David in the late 1800's, they were there, holding court. There was nowhere to hide, to pull Olivia another direction away from them.

The blue humor of the night before at the café continued, with endless comments about the size of David's penis. Families stood nearby, trying to look at the sculpture with their children, likely a planned highlight of the trip to Florence to show their kids one of the greatest pieces by one of the most famous artists. But instead, children were ushered away by frustrated parents, another moment of another family trip ruined. I felt bad for them, embarrassed for them. My experience was being tarnished as well. The quiet moments of listening to Olivia speak so passionately about what she loved was being taken away.

I tried to engage Olivia again, to get her back into art history mode to tell me about the creation and history of the work, but she was pulled in once again by the couple.

"They're funny," she said.

"She doesn't say anything, and he isn't that clever."

"Oh, come on. I want to talk to them."

"Absolutely not." I looked over at the man at entirely the wrong moment and locked eyes with him.

"Am I not right!" the man yelled, seemingly at me.

I turned my head, but it was too late, like catching the eye of a stand-up comic at an amateur open mic night. You were then his foil, the butt of unfunny jokes to come, no matter what you did.

He moved across the room until he was standing next to me, a long arm went around my shoulder and pulled me in, so we were side by side facing the David. A blast of body odor struck my nose from his raised arm and I stifled a gag.

"Is it not tiny?" he said, seeming to exaggerate his already thick Italian accent. "If the statue was brought to normal height it would be *molto piccolo*."

He reached his arm up, thumb and forefinger extending to size the statue's member from a distance, then moved it down to his own crotch, scaling it down as he went, until it was maybe a centimeter long. With this he turned to the woman with him and moved his hips in and out with the simulated penis size ramming into her. She laughed. Olivia laughed. A few teenagers laughed. Parents pulled their young children away in disgust.

I wanted to walk away, but Olivia had engaged with them. The man kissed her cheeks, as did the woman with him, when she introduced herself and they found out we were American. "Oh, how I love Americans!" he proclaimed louder than he needed. She gave them my name as I tried to walk away, pretending to be staring at the sculpture.

"I am Giuseppe," the man said. "But friends call me Pippo. This is my ravenous girlfriend, my muse, my reason for being, Scarlet." With that introduction he then kissed Scarlet in a manner I was certain would turn into intercourse right there in the Tribunal room. When they finally parted lips, his hand was still wrapped around her body, hand grabbing her ass through the thin red dress with white polka dots. She was shorter than her partner, the top of her head at his shoulder height and all I could think about was how could she tolerate the stink of his armpits, her nose only inches away.

My mind worked through every scenario I could for escape, but for someone who creates stories for a living, I could come up with no way to get out of this situation. No ending I could conjure seemed believable for a reader. I could only hope that Olivia would tire of them quickly.

The man suggested leaving the museum and Olivia said yes before I was even sure I'd heard the question. As much as I wanted away from them, I also had compassion for the other visitors and endorsed the idea.

Behind the couple at the exit I leaned down to Olivia's ear and whispered, "You owe me."

She looked back at me with a smile that made many promises. A ten-minute walk later and we were drinking at a café, sitting outside in the heat.

Pippo and Scarlet were in constant body contact, hands stroking thighs or rubbing the other's back. I sweat more just thinking about it. As much as I loved Olivia, I wanted nothing extra on my body until I had cooled off and probably showered.

I sat on the periphery of conversation, doing my best to ignore him while trying to keep from getting caught looking at Scarlet. It was difficult. Each time I glanced her way she seemed to be looking at me. Olivia was laughing too hard to notice.

"What brings the two of you to Florence?" Scarlet was looking at me, trying to pull me in. She had an accent I couldn't place. Olivia answered.

"Just a vacation. I studied here in college years ago and wanted to come back, so Avery brought me."

Pippo leaned across the table and slapped my shoulder harder than he needed to.

"That is a good man who knows how to treat his lover," he said. "Treat her well, and she will treat you well." He winked an exaggerated wink, meant to be seen by everyone, to highlight his not so subtle innuendo.

My shoulder still tingled from the slap and my dislike of him was edging toward hatred.

"Where are you from?" Olivia directed her question at Scarlet.

"Amsterdam," she said. "Actually, a smaller town further south called Leiden, but I moved to Amsterdam for work. That's where I met Pippo."

Pippo put his hand behind Scarlet's neck and roughly

pulled her in. She smiled as he did and kissed him, her hand going to his chest and under the shirt unbuttoned too far.

"That was the most amazing night ever," he said once they had released each other. "I am not one to believe in fate, do you know? But that night, I did."

"What happened?" Olivia was too energetic in her response, knowing full well they were going to tell us.

"I was in Amsterdam with some friends. They got drunk and went off to the red-light district. I had no interest in whores, so I stayed back and decided to walk around, have some drinks alone, perhaps meet a woman I did not have to pay. I found myself on a dark road and was jumped by several young men, boys really, teenagers. They stole my wallet and my cellphone, even the key to my hotel room."

"Oh, no!" Olivia responded as if reading a script.

"I was not hurt, just shaken up, as you say. I found my way back to a street with some shops and there I walked into a store to ask for help, to use the telephone."

"I was behind the counter and saw him come in," Scarlet took over. "He looked lost and confused. I asked if he needed help, and he said he did. I gave him my cellphone to make a call." It was the most I'd heard her say at once.

"Then I realized I did not know who to call." Pippo interrupted her, a hand going up in front of her face. "I was thinking the whole time as I tried to find a place to go, I need to call someone, but once I had a phone, I did not know who."

"It was almost time for the shop to close, so he waited, and I took him to the *gendarmerie*, the police. He told them what happened, but we could tell they weren't too concerned."

A sideways glance from Pippo, eager to take the spotlight again. "She walked with me back to my hotel and said goodbye," Pippo said. "Luckily I had money and my passport in my room. I travel often and know not to carry everything with me. I never have much cash, only credit cards. The thieves would be able to do nothing with the one they stole. Maybe they got a few dollars for the phone."

More drinks were ordered. I didn't object. It dulled the pain of being with them and dare I say, made it almost enjoyable when I was buzzed. My participation in the conversation was passive, a bystander at the same table, in a state of limbo between enjoying myself and walking away. I watched the people who moved around us, others at the café or walking past. I was distracted by any sparkly item that pulled me away.

"The next day," Pippo continued after the break as if it had been one singular breath. "I wake up and am so thankful for this beautiful woman who had helped me, been so compassionate, whose name I never learned. I went out to look for her, to try to find the shop she worked in, but I did not know what it was called. I walked for hours, circling blocks and looking at every store, but it looked different in the daylight. I see a shop on a corner with a pink awning, and it is familiar. I go in and I ask if a beautiful black princess with the purest heart works there. A woman tells me she does but will not be in for another hour. I go for a walk, checking the time on my watch constantly, eager to see her again."

He extends his arm to unnecessarily recreate his actions in a motion not professional enough for a junior high summer theater camp. A Rolex reflected the sunlight before disappearing beneath his shirtsleeve again.

"This is so romantic!" Olivia said.

"I walk through the door, and there she is behind the counter just like the night before," Pippo says. "She looks up at me and smiles, then said—" he turns his body to her, granting permission to finish the story.

"Did you get robbed again?" Scarlet finished the sentence and they both laughed.

"She was a beautiful vision, so sweet and innocent looking," he said. "I was certain in that moment I was falling in love with her and I didn't even know her name yet."

"I was quite taken with him, as well," Scarlet said. "I had been captivated by his personality, of course his looks, and his musk the night before."

I gagged a little.

"That is such an incredible story, you two!" Olivia said.

"I never went back to the shop," Scarlet said. "He asked me to join him, and I did."

"What kind of shop was it?" I said.

"A sex store, you know," Pippo said. "Like dildos and stuff."

CHAPTER ELEVEN

The avocado green dress contrasts the grey stone ground and walls surrounding it. I am so focused on the beauty of the color I don't realize it is Sara until I am almost standing over her. The dress is similar to the one she wore last night except for the color. Thin straps go over the shoulders, exposing her arms and back. She sits under an umbrella at a table outside a café, sipping from a tall glass. I stop and watch as her red hair bounces with the light breeze. It's the newness of it, I'm sure. The sudden attention from a pretty woman. But I'm drawn to her. It's more than sexual. It's sweet and caring. It's laughter and fun. *Fun.* I haven't had fun in a long time.

"You look incredible."

She glances up at me, her eyes taking me in from top to bottom followed by a catcall whistle.

"You look quite handsome yourself," she says, looking at my new suit.

"You like? I just picked it up this morning."

"I do like."

I sit and her hand moves over to take mine. *Comfort.* My palm is sweaty immediately but I don't care and she doesn't seem to, either.

"What do you want to do this evening?" I motion for the waitress.

She sips her drink, which is a little muddy with mint leaves.

"I had thought about going to the *Accadamie*, it's open late tonight, but then I decided I just want to be somewhere we can talk, drink, eat, then go home and make love all night."

Home. The word sticks out for the eventual briefness of our relationship, but it sounds good. The thought of having a home with someone, even if just for a couple of nights, invigorates me. It contradicts everything about the trip, my intentions. My house in Kansas where I've slept the last year seems nothing more than that, a place to rest.

"I think that's the plan, then."

The waitress comes by and I tell her two more of what she's having. Sara moves her chair a little closer to mine.

"How was your shower?" I say.

"Lonely."

"If yours is anything like the one in my apartment, then they are designed for lonely showers."

"I barely fit in mine."

I lean in and kiss her, the first of many times for the day. I linger on her lips, wonderfully soft and inviting, a hint of mint and rum. She doesn't pull away, staying in that moment with me. I've found nothing more personal than a kiss. Sex is intimate, physical. But a kiss is face to face, eye to eye. It's the risk of bad breath or rough lips. Obtrusive tongues when you don't like that or not enough if you do. Couples that like the same kissing tend to kiss often. For everyone else it's only a goodbye/hello and a suggestion for sex, the sign you are in the mood and interested in something more right then. In our one night and one morning together, we've kissed a lot. When we do, I feel her quiver, a shortened breath, and realize I am doing the same.

"So, you leave tomorrow."

"I'm not sure yet." I pause. I want to see her more but it is distracting me from following him, from building up my courage to confront him, getting my answers. "But I'm probably here at least one more night."

Her smile radiates through me. I try to think of a way to continue my quest while still spending time with her. I know the places Olivia and I went with the couple a year ago, but it would seem suspicious if we end up in the same place as them again, wouldn't it? But again, Florence is not a large city. I glance at my watch.

"Are you hungry?" I say.

"I am."

I settle the bill. We stand, she puts her arm through mine, and we walk. It's a crazy idea, but it is all I can figure to do. I have the mission of following Pippo, getting closer and closer until I confront, but then I have the draw of a beautiful woman pulling me away. I rationalize the evening by thinking I don't stand out as much dining with a young woman as I would alone. At least for now. For tonight.

The nights we'd spent in Florence with Pippo, I'd learned his favorite restaurant. We ate there three times. He knew all of the waitresses by name and had ordered for everyone, family style. It isn't something fancy and overpriced with a chef whose name is known across Italy. It's one of those Italian restaurants with long tables meant for groups or for strangers to get to know each other whether they want to or not. It is old and out of the way, meant for locals, and smells of the garlic that hangs in large cloves from the walls. More food than we could eat would be served on those nights, and by the end it was all gone.

The restaurant is mostly empty tonight, or we're just too early for the crowds. We arrive and sit at the far end of a table away from the few other people, close to the door, defying the waves of the friendly older woman who runs the place trying to seat us near other people. I want an escape route, a view over the room. Sara probably thinks I want to sit alone with her, which is also true. Food is ordered along with a bottle of wine. I don't feel I have to watch for him, certain he will make his presence known to everyone if he comes.

Olivia and I had come here with them the next night after meeting at the *Accadamie*. I resisted, but not too hard as I knew she wanted to go. She was amused by them, and I liked to make her happy. We drank into the night, occupying a table in the middle of the restaurant for hours. Others came and went around us, pulled in by Pippo, then were released when someone more interesting would take their place in his favor. When the night was over, I had no idea who paid the check, but taxis were called and Olivia and I had made it back to our apartment. There wasn't a day or evening we didn't spend with them for the rest of the trip.

Conversation is easy with Sara. We don't ask many questions about each other's past. No deep dives into family history or exes. It is more about today and now and often times sexual. She admits to not being very experienced. I tell her the same. That's as personal as we get, aside from sharing each other's bodies fully and openly with each other.

"How long are you planning on living in Florence?"

She looks past me at nothing as she considers the question. "I'm not sure yet."

"Missing Ireland too much?"

"My family, yes, but the weather, no. I think I always want to be somewhere sunny. Somewhere warm. I would like to be near the ocean, I think." She bites her lower lip while looking me in the eyes. "I've actually looked into the office in Los Angeles before."

It takes a moment to click what she means. "Oh, really? It is always sunny." I don't know what to say.

"It was before we met, of course. I'm not a total lunatic. Maybe I could come for a visit, to check out the offices sometime?"

I nod and force a smile. "That would be great." The lies are already catching up to me.

The looming end of the affair is ever present, but neither of us let it bring us down. I do want to know her better. Maybe another time. *After.* I have to either tell her the truth or disappear from her life completely. Perhaps when this is over I can meet her in Los Angeles, come clean about who I am, where I'm from. Kansas City doesn't hold the allure that California does, and it would be easier to run from her if I wasn't at home.

Pasta is served, placed in front of us with no flare, the food speaking for itself. It is handmade in the kitchen, the meats and cheeses sourced locally. Nothing we consume comes from further than twenty miles from Florence. The *pici* on my plate is wound into a tower of pasta, a sea of red sauce around it. The *saltimbocca,* a merging of veal, prosciutto, and herbs, delights her.

We finish eating and the rest of the house Chianti is poured into our glasses. She doesn't turn her nose up sipping the deep red liquid as much, getting used to the heavy wines.

"I like this." She takes my hand from across the table.

"Me too." Too much.

The restaurant is still quiet. A few other people are eating but the voices are low, white noise barely heard across the room. No sign of Pippo and Scarlet. I consider getting us out, moving on to my apartment and more wine. But I know I can't let her distract me. I suggest dessert, she agrees.

Tiramisu is served and devoured. I'm feeling loose from the wine and aroused from looking at Sara all night and imagine touching her. I pay the check.

"I wish to take your clothes off of you now," I say.

"I wish to let you."

Sara comes around the end of the table and takes my hand I hold out for her. She kisses me. I smile as I think about us acting like teenagers on a date, grinning and giggling, taking every opportunity to stop and kiss, to fondle. We won't be relegated to the back seat of a borrowed minivan or an old sofa in a basement, one ear always listening for the door to open and an angry father storming in to catch us in the act.

I take a step and feel the full effects of the better part of two bottles of wine. She had maybe two glasses, the rest was all me and I'm past tipsy.

The man outside responsible for driving people into the restaurant opens the door and stands back, thanking us on our way through.

"*Grazi*," I look back and say too loudly, my head swimming, my steps unsure as I receive the full impact of the drink once my blood flows quicker from walking. As I turn to look ahead of me, I slam into a man, full body on body, making us both stagger backwards away from each other. The man drops his cellphone and is swearing in Italian as he picks it up and checks the screen. I know before I can even see his face. His shape. His smell.

Pippo.

I stand motionless, willing my body to act, to move on. I stare as he checks himself up and down to ensure he is not injured, scuffed, or altered in any other way, before he looks up at me. Our eyes meet for a moment as Sara asks him if he is okay. My voice is gone, stolen by the moment, unable to make a sound. He waves an arm without even looking at her, dismissing her, the situation.

"Yes, yes. I am fine." His head tilts and he moves on, more words muttered in Italian as he goes, followed by a sudden change of mood, a cheerful greeting to the doorman. "*Ciao*, Nicola!" The two faces of Pippo I know so well.

I find a way to move again, taking a step, then another. Sara is talking and like last night, I'm not hearing her. I was face to face with him, touched him. I could still smell his sweat. Even if I hadn't seen his face, I would know him by his stench. He looked in my eyes but I couldn't tell if he recognized me. If he did, what does that mean? Scarlet hadn't been with him or she surely would have seen who I was. A thinner body and a beard only go so far in disguising a person.

"Was that the guy from last night?" Sara's voice comes through. "The loud guy from the café?"

The wine is still working on my brain, slowing thoughts down.

"Pippo," I mutter. An unfiltered reaction. A thought that became verbalized.

"What?"

I realize what I said and managed to stop myself from saying it again. "Nothing."

"Pippo? What's that?"

I grab her arm and turn her away from the restaurant, from the doorman who might know his name. "No, I said people. Some people are just rude."

"But I think you bumped into him."

I try to push it away. "The same guy? Was it?"

"I think it was."

"What a coincidence." I walk us to the next corner and flag a taxi that was coming toward us. I'm rattled. Confused. "Would you like to go for more drinks somewhere, or—"

"I want to go home and take your clothes off of you."

Home.

"I'm all for that."

CHAPTER TWELVE

One evening with Pippo and Scarlet had turned into a second, which went on into the night. It continued that way for a week. Each evening was a different bar, a different audience. But each involved copious amounts of wine, and watching Pippo and Scarlet come close to having sex in public.

As events happen, you don't usually note them for their importance. They seem like another night, another drink. When you look back, you can begin to identify the quantum shifts in what is considered real or normal. What you have accepted your entire life can be altered, momentum changed with a left turn instead of a right, ordering Prosecco instead of red wine.

The night had begun like those before it. Olivia and I met them at a restaurant where dinner turned to drinks, then more drinks. We walked to other bars and took a taxi across the river to a club Pippo knew about, only to find it out of business. That didn't slow him down. A café down the street was open and we took up residence at the tables out front. Two bottles of wine were ordered which emptied faster than I knew possible for four people drinking.

"Avery, what do you do back in, where is it, Oklahoma?" Pippo said.

"Kansas."

"Ahh, right. Kansas." His pronunciation of the state reeked of sarcasm.

"I teach literature at a college."

Olivia put her arm through mine and pulled herself closer. "And he writes books."

I had sensed it coming and turned to try to stop her, but it was too late.

"His books are very successful," she said. "You have, what, twenty out?"

"Twenty-three." I withdrew, tried to think of a way to redirect, change the subject, not wanting to have that conversation. I kept that part of my life private. Nobody at my college even knew about them. A literature professor writing juvenile whodunits. I'd be ridiculed.

"A famous author? Here with us?" Pippo was intrigued. "What have you written? Tell me about them."

My stomach tightened.

"They're children's books," Olivia said. "Mysteries."

Pippo's brow furled in confusion. "What kind of mysteries are written for children?"

Olivia was eager to talk about them. "Like detective stories. There's three children, two girls and a boy, and they help their friends find stolen or missing objects."

"And you make money off of these stories?"

I nod. Being with Pippo and Scarlet was at the same time draining and exhilarating. My dislike of him was still there. He was an overly gregarious and obnoxious man. If you weren't in his favor, then you were the object of his ridicule, which in turn made you want to be liked by him. But wine flowed easily when near him, and the bill never ended up in my hand. Even in college I hadn't drunk as much as I did each night with them.

There'd been something about him that kept me defensive, on edge, as if at any time he could have blown up. Through the laughter and wine, it was ever-present, waiting to show itself. A tension. An anger, perhaps.

Scarlet was the opposite of her partner. While sociable and outgoing, she was also kind and sweet. Don't get me wrong, I was there with the woman I loved, but Scarlet was magnetic. I caught myself watching her, craving her. She always looked incredible, hair in the right place, makeup perfect while not looking like she was wearing any at all. Her mixed race Kenyan and Dutch heritage combined into a flawless and unique beauty. When she spoke to you, you felt she wanted to be right there, nowhere else, only sharing those words at that moment no matter what was going on around you. In a moment of weakness, my thoughts had gone to her back at the apartment while making love with Olivia the night before. There was nothing pure about the thoughts, no longing for being with her other than for a night of sex, a moment of release, a lust for feeling her on me.

I grew up in a town that was ignorantly proud of its whiteness, of its racism. When I was a child a young man was sent to town along with his wife to run the Sears catalog store, a location with a few appliances in stock to buy but mostly you ordered from their catalog in person. I saw them once at the grocery store and they stood out in the cereal aisle. Dark skin contrasted with white linoleum floors. Other people walked the opposite direction, not wanting to be near them, lest they accidentally breathe the same air. Not so subtle whispers from the cookie aisle that I'm sure they overheard. I was only eleven or twelve but thought his wife was beautiful, something from the movies I'd watch on TBS on Sunday mornings. I thought about her often and desired glimpses of her in town the short time they lived there. They moved suddenly on a Tuesday. A strange day to move, I always thought. The Sears store remained closed, though the sign said they should be open. They threw what possessions they could from their small rented house into the back of a Toyota hatchback and drove out of town faster than was legal, or so the triumphant stories went. The police didn't even pull them over. They sat on the side of the road and watched them leave, lights flashing on their roofs. It wasn't until years later I heard more stories, about men in white hoods going to their house late on a Monday night. When these stories were told, there was laughter.

The café closed, leaving us homeless again. Pippo insisted we all go back to their apartment where a fully stocked bar and wine cabinet awaited. The decision was made easily and we went. It was a huge space for

Florence with two large suites on either side of an open living area and a balcony over the street two floors down. It had a private entrance with a grand stairwell leading up to the residence in a private vestibule, like nothing I'd seen in Italy, or even at home. We were barely through the door when the first bottles of Prosecco were opened and glasses handed around.

The mood was different, more subdued without the potential for others to overhear our conversation, for Pippo to entertain. His brashness was diminished, though not entirely gone. He craved to be evocative, trying to shock with each word spoken. Scarlet was a natural at softening his tone, turning the conversation elsewhere. While he was distracted with her body lounging against his, she turned to us.

"How much longer are you in Florence?" Scarlet said.

"Another ten days, I think, but I'm trying not to think about going home yet." Olivia was curled up with me on the small sofa opposite the matching one where Pippo and Scarlet sat, her leaning against his body, one of his arms wrapped around her. His right hand held a glass, the other held Scarlet's left breast over her dress with a constant, slow movement, caressing, cupping. I sensed Olivia's hesitation while speaking, taken back by watching him touch her so openly.

"I wanted Avery to really experience Florence like a local. I know two weeks doesn't really qualify, but it was the best we could do. He has the summer off, but I have to get back to work."

Scarlet turned her head and kissed Pippo. Tongues lingered, stroking lips, as his hand continued its slow, circling massage of her breast.

"Of everywhere I have been," Pippo said, his face barely separated from Scarlet's, his breath spreading across her as he spoke. "I have always found sex in Florence the most pleasing. More sensual, hedonic. Animalistic. Something deep inside my soul takes over, perhaps a trait left over from before we became civilized."

I didn't know how to respond or if I was supposed to. It seemed a private conversation in front of us, his eyes still locked onto hers, his hand still attached to her breast.

"I do not know if it is the air or the wine, or just the history and the sexuality of the artists who lived here, walked these streets, created masterpieces in oil and words in these spaces."

As he spoke, his hand slid up to the bare skin above Scarlet's dress, fingers spread wide, pushing under the edge of the fabric, and went back down to her braless chest under the almost transparent white dress while their eyes never left each other's. His hand embraced her breast, then fingers took her nipple between them and Scarlet let out the lightest gasp when he squeezed. We were now their audience, voyeurs with permission.

"Dante was thought to live in this very building," he continued. "To think words may have been written right where you are sitting that are studied in universities around the world, that you might discuss in your Kansas classroom." He never turned to look at me, but brought me into his narrative, making me an accomplice to his actions. My eyes couldn't leave his fingers on her breast beneath the thin layer of cloth, which hid nothing.

Scarlet turned and straightened her body against his, an arm raised and grabbed his head as they kissed, clutching his perfect hair. The new position gave Pippo access to slide his hand farther down. The shape of his arm inside the dress was a sculpted relief in motion, a serpent-like slithering between her breasts, across her stomach. Her back arched as he touched her where I was already certain she was wearing no panties beneath the dress. The smoothness of the material across her ass as we walked from café to café convinced me of that fact earlier in the evening, keeping my attention on her shape while trying to avoid anyone noticing my distracted gaze.

I could feel Olivia beside me, her motion, her heat. Her body moved slowly in the way I knew she did when excited. Visibly she was frozen. It was subtle, glacial speeds not noticeable unless you were in bodily contact with her as I was. I wanted to cross my legs to hide my own growing excitement, but Olivia's position wrapped up in my arm didn't allow it.

We could do nothing but watch as he manipulated her with his hand, her body writhing against his, her tongue on his face and neck. There was nothing I could find to say, no conversation to offer. The room was his, just as he preferred, to control and preside over in whatever way he liked, and right now that was to make his girlfriend climax in front of us, controlling her body as if it belonged to him.

Olivia's motion became more exaggerated as her body gave in to the excitement of watching the couple. Her hand moved several times up the smooth skin of her own leg, stopping just under the edge of her dress as she caught herself, not yet willing to go to the lengths of our hosts.

A whimper across from us, Scarlet reacting to another movement, a touch, a penetration, perhaps. She reached down between Pippo's legs and rubbed him, her hand outlining the firmness below the expensive linen he always wore. As if synchronized, her hand undid the button on his slacks, releasing him, as he pulled her dress up, exposing her bare body. Both Olivia and I froze though it shouldn't have been unexpected. Scarlet had her mouth on him as he continued to pleasure her manually.

We watched in stunned silence, only the sounds of their bodies occupying the air. I moved my hand to try to hide myself, still unable to fathom what was happening before us. Pippo pulled Scarlet's dress up and over her head, leaving her naked six feet from us, as her mouth continued to work him.

Olivia couldn't take any more. Her hands came to my body, grabbing my shirt as she kissed me. It was only moments before her short dress was raised and she was sitting on my lap, her hand undoing my slacks and putting me inside of her. I didn't argue or resist, or take my eyes off of Scarlet's skin. Olivia kept turning her head to see them. I spun her left and put her on the silk sofa with brightly colored intricate patterns woven into it. *Fleur-de-lis.* I entered her again as we both looked across to them and I moved slowly to control the pace but she wanted more. She wanted harder.

Scarlet was now on top of Pippo, heads facing opposite directions, mouths creating pleasure for each other. As she moved on him, her eyes came over and locked with mine. Olivia shook with the momentum I unconsciously exerted in that moment, my body reacting to the desire I had felt for Scarlet, now seeing her with another man in her mouth. A few seconds later Olivia's body tightened, nerve endings reached capacity, and she came. I slowed again. Her hands were on my chest and I thrust myself deeper, then stopped, holding myself inside her as far as I could as I climaxed then collapsed onto her.

I held her, both of us silent as we looked at each other, minds wrapping around the moment. We heard Scarlet's breathing get louder, faster, and a series of staccato whimpers that grew to near a scream. In an unspoken agreement we turned our heads to watch as Scarlet came, me still inside Olivia, Scarlet looking at me as she did.

The room hung in suspended time. The sounds of bodies enjoying themselves was gone, breathing returned to normal. Skin still sweaty. My pants were at my knees while I was still surrounded by Olivia, unsure what to do, how to move from our awkward position.

"Who wants more wine?" The silence didn't last as Pippo stood up, his long, thin, now flaccid penis in full view as he placed himself back into his pants while facing us as casually as if he were straightening a handkerchief in his pocket or zipping a jacket. Scarlet got up, pulling her dress back over her body, completely nude standing in front of us for a moment as she did, leaving us exposed on the other sofa.

"I definitely do," Olivia said.

I stood and she did the same, pulling my slacks up as she lowered her dress and attempted to smooth the wrinkles out with her hands. I see Scarlet looking at me as I place myself back into my underwear then zip. Her eyes move from my crotch to my eyes. She smiles then turns away to help Pippo with the wine.

Glasses were handed around whether you said you wanted more or not, and conversation continued as if nothing had happened, that two couples hadn't just had sex at the same time in the same room.

Music was turned on. Pippo and Scarlet slow danced to an Italian song that was familiar from some old film or the music playing overhead in a café at which we'd eaten once. Or maybe an Olive Garden in Kansas City.

Even in the minutes after making love, their amorous behavior didn't slow. His hands worked her body as they danced, taking in every curve and detail. Then he stopped with Scarlet in mid turn and looked at us.

"What day is this?" he said.

"It's Wednesday." I looked at Olivia for confirmation. "I think." She nodded.

Pippo grabbed Scarlet again and spun her, looped

her under his arm and ended up in a dip, none of the motions matching the rhythm of the song.

"Then we will go to the sea this weekend!" Pippo said.

"Yes! Yes!" Scarlet screamed. Her hands went into the air like a contestant on *The Price is Right* who was just called to come down to the front of the stage. She jumped and wrapped her legs around his body, her dress pulling back up to expose her ass once again. I couldn't help but look and didn't try to hide it.

"What do you mean?" Olivia said.

"The sea!" Scarlet screamed again. "*Il mare!*"

"I have an apartment in Positano," Pippo said. "We haven't been down in months. What do you say?"

"I…" I had no answer to the spontaneous question.

"Yes!" Olivia responded.

I looked over at her and saw her smile, her excitement at the thought.

"Sure," I said.

"It is settled then," Pippo said. "We leave Friday morning. I will make the arrangements for transportation."

Tredici
CHAPTER THIRTEEN

My back was to her when we woke the next morning in the guest suite at Pippo's apartment. No playful pretend sleeping. Positano should have been on my mind but instead it was guilt. Guilt from doing what we had done, from looking at another woman, from wanting another woman. Wanting Scarlet.

Her hand came around my chest, fingers spreading wide to touch as much of me as possible. I could feel her warm breath on my neck as her naked body connected with mine.

"You okay?" Her voice tickled my ear with its softness.

"Yeah."

"You don't seem okay." Her hand stroked my skin. "I don't mind, you know."

"Mind what?"

"That you watched her. That you look at her."

I hadn't known what to say and was glad I was facing away from her, only the white wall in my vision to judge me. In all my subtlety I'd thought she hadn't noticed, except for the night before when we were all looking at each other's naked bodies.

"She's gorgeous. It's okay to look."

"You know I only care about you."

I could feel her face against my neck move to a smile. "I do. But there's no harm in looking at beautiful people."

I rolled over and looked at her wonderful face, her warm eyes. "Can we be alone today? Just you and me?"

Her smile answered.

We left the apartment before our hosts had awakened, and freshened up at our place, followed swiftly by making love, our bodies still wet from the shower, still aroused from the night before. My attention was all on her.

I wanted out of town for a few hours, a break from the city even with the impending trip to the sea. I was exhausted thinking about it. Three straight days with them.

A car was rented from an agency by the train station, and we left Florence behind us for the day.

I drove for an hour on small winding roads, avoiding the bigger highways as the perfect blue above was slowly replaced by ever darkening clouds. The stone towers of San Gimignano came into view, contrasted against the approaching blue and black storm that provided the backdrop.

We parked to find refuge and food within the city walls. Tourists lined up at the shop beside the main gate buying coffee and snacks. We walked past them into the village.

The rain began not far into town. Large, heavy drops that fell slowly, making their collision with the ground more dramatic, exploding with loud plops.

We walked on the edge of the rough stone road to let the buildings block most of the rain. She grabbed my arm and pulled me down an alley as it turned to a steady shower. An old Vespa sat covered with years of dirt in the shadows of the narrow lane, unused after the engine probably died and the owner couldn't fix it or afford to have it repaired.

We continued on, making turns through the deepest parts of the narrow town until she saw a stairwell ahead. *Come on. Up there!* At the top was a balcony overlooking the valley to the left and the town to the right, and partly covered to keep us protected from most of the rain that only became stronger with each passing moment. We took the stairs two at a time and were out of breath when we reached the top.

I wrapped her in my arms and held her tight from behind as we looked out at the ever-threatening sky. Flashes lit the horizon, diffused by clouds making the heavens explode in bursts of light, followed by a long, low rumble. I counted the seconds between lightning and thunder as I had when I was a child, to see how far away the center of the storm was while we stood there watching the tremendous black clouds roll across the landscape. Three seconds between. A few minutes later only two seconds. Until finally the thunder and lightning hit at the same time when the full force of the storm was over the medieval town.

The thunder was unlike anything I ever heard before. Each time it lasted for minutes, as if a large truck was rolling toward me, shaking the road and my skin and my ears as it grew louder and louder until fading off into nothingness, leaving an unnatural silence in its wake. Lightning struck nearby, a cracking sound from a tree echoed across the valley below the high wall. And still the thunder, never ending in its crusade, rattled the earth below as a warning, a deep bass felt in my chest.

We'd stood there witnessing the storm, spectators to a battle between gods. The air had cooled and bristled our skin with each gust of wind. My arms wrapped tighter around Olivia as if to protect her, or soothe myself. She was my safety blanket, my pacifier.

I felt the vibration through the air and Olivia's skin against mine. It joined us together, fused our cells in those moments the thunder sounded above us, around us. I never knew if she felt it, too, or if I imagined the connection, the alignment of our molecules from the static electricity surrounding our bodies.

In that thunderstorm in an ancient village, rain pelting the ledge in front of us and ricocheting up to wet our clothes, I fell in love with her. The words had been said many times by both of us in late night sweaty embraces, in early morning relaxation with the sun pouring in over us, and while walking down busy streets looking in windows and eating at quiet cafés. I had already told her I loved her, and had believed I did, but it was there surrounded by that storm that I knew it was true. Wet and cold from the rain, humbled from the majesty of the scene before us, I wanted to be with her forever.

A future flashed before me of holding hands and smiles, making love and sharing a home. A child and then another and just pure happiness. Our lives took shape in microseconds. Things I never knew I wanted or could have. Emotions that were foreign to me.

There was no grand gesture made. I didn't go down on my knee, fashioning a ring with our receipt from cappuccino that morning until something proper could be purchased. I just kept holding her and she kept holding me back while the rain continued to wet our bodies. But I knew that was our future, that the gesture would be made, the question asked, and I knew that she would say yes. Anything we had was strong enough to handle nights out drinking with Pippo and Scarlet, a weekend with them on the Amalfi Coast. Olivia knew I loved her and only her and casual gazes at another beautiful woman took nothing away from that.

As the storm moved on from San Gimignano, we reluctantly abandoned our perch. Many shops were closed. The lightning had knocked out electricity to half the town. One side of the street was dark while shops on the other side cast an unnatural glow into the air and onto the wet stones. A light rain continued so we took a table in the window of a café. We drank wine while we watched the tourists clamor for umbrellas being sold for five euros each that had been three before the storm. Before long, the street was lined with pink, yellow, and green canopies that would break before making their trips home.

The sky was clearing as we left the town. The tourists had all fled. By the time we walked down the hill to our car, now alone in the large parking lot, the sun was shining again, casting brilliant light across the valley, shades of gold sprawled out before us. Once in the warm car, she leaned her head over onto my shoulder and I felt her body relax.

"I'm not ready to go back," she said.

"Me too."

We set out to get lost on the winding backroads. The rolling hills of Tuscany pulled the car along, urging us to see what was over the next rise, around the next curve. The view was never disappointing. Signs for Siena came and went and we kept going, just driving through the country, content in the silence and warmth of the rented car.

Getting lost is wonderful when done properly. You never want to run out of gas or be too far away from civilization in case anything should go wrong. In the modern day of cellphones it is almost impossible ever to be somewhere you cannot be found, especially if you are on a road. Being lost is more a state of mind, allowing yourself to not look at the maps that are always at your fingertips. The key is not knowing where you are going and not caring about when you get there.

Guided tours leave no room for exploration. You know before you ever depart your home where you will be sleeping, where you will be eating, and how you are getting from one place to another. Itineraries are printed on glossy paper and mailed to your home a month ahead of time, every minute accounted for. It is comforting to some, to have everything taken care of for you, to not have to think. I would have been like that had Olivia not planned this trip. She didn't have us moving town to town to see everything on the Top 10 list of things to do in Tuscany, packing our bags every morning for the migration to another village, another hotel.

A strict schedule keeps you from finding the time to wander. You walk right past every shop and café without a thought about what wondrous things might be in there, because at 2:45 you're supposed to be back on the bus to the next predetermined destination and restaurant that caters to forty guests at a time with a *prix fixe* menu identical to the one from the night before in a different town. We had seen the hordes of tourists being led through Florence, cheap headphones relaying the voice of their tour guide in broken English of the most clichéd sights to see.

The sun was low in the sky when we stopped in Montalcino for dinner. From the side of the ancient castle at the top of the town we watched out over the golden fields as they grew deeper in color as darkness overtook the land, golds into browns, then blacks.

"*Val d'Orcia*," she said. "I never made it down here. It's just..."

"Perfect."

"Yeah."

We left town and drove down into the vastness we'd watched fall into night. The narrow roads pulled in tighter as the headlights on the small car cast their glow across the overgrown flora lining the edges of the road, blocking our view except for the occasional opening offering glimpses of wide-open fields.

At one curve a lane continued forward, only used by those who knew of its existence. A driver needed the faith not to turn the steering wheel, instead seeming to fly out over the fields to find it. I'd been driving slowly, in no hurry and to keep the car on the pavement, and saw it out of the corner of my eye while curving right. Without a hesitation I yanked the wheel onto the loose gravel road.

Olivia never jumped or asked where I was going. She was relaxed beside me, trusting in whatever course I chose and followed.

There was no overgrowth on the sides of the lane and our view opened up. I let off the gas without thinking and we rolled to a stop.

"Turn off the lights," she said.

We fell into blackness until pupils adjusted and the light coming from above gave us vision again. I turned the engine off and the night swallowed us in silence, engulfed us. She was out of the car first and I followed. With every second, every step, things around us came into view, shadows and silhouettes dotted the landscape.

"I always thought that Kansas had the biggest sky," I said. "But I'd just never really seen it anywhere else." My voice was out of place, too loud for the surroundings, too crass to be heard in this solitude.

"I don't think I've ever really looked up until tonight." Olivia whispered but I heard every word. She exhaled and took in the night air.

With no hills to block the view in Kansas, I'd lie on the hood of my car in the country and stare up at the sky at night when I was younger. It was an escape from whatever was happening in my real world. High school and exams, college applications. When Olivia and I stood in Tuscany together looking up, the stars above filled the sky, leaving few voids in space. Constellations stood out in the randomness of suns burning so far away.

My feelings of insignificance from looking up at the stars in my childhood was gone. Instead I felt connected to something far greater than myself, greater than anything I could ever accomplish. A knowledge comes with the universe expanding in front of you, of realizing that no one person is more important than any other, no matter their net worth or title. Everything works together. The ants below us are no less significant than the moon above, or the planets beyond it. The moment you understand this, everything changes. Your future seems less daunting, difficult tasks you'd put off feel simple or unimportant.

The impossible part is maintaining this knowledge, keeping it in the front of your mind once the world around you becomes small again. Once you are back home paying bills, grocery shopping, working, it retreats from your memory, leaving only a shadow of something you once knew. Sometimes it slips into your conscious thoughts just as you are falling asleep, that sense of some greater meaning, only to be gone again in the morning.

I wanted to always remember the stars that night and how I'd shared them with Olivia. No photograph I could take would capture them properly. I put my arms around her and kissed her.

"I love you."

Her body leaned into mine, her head on my shoulder. "I love you, too."

We looked up at the stars again before leaving. The headlights waited eagerly to make them vanish before our eyes. I wanted to look into the night sky with her again someday soon, to share the night with her, to see the stars once more.

Olivia fell asleep beside me on the ride back to Florence, only waking when we came to a stop at the rental car return. She looked around as if waking from a hundred-night slumber and took in her surroundings, ending at me with a smile and a kiss on my cheek.

We slept well that night. It was a comfort of knowing each other fully, accepting each other, and wanting to be together, as our new-found knowledge faded with sleep.

CHAPTER FOURTEEN

Sara sleeps while I dress quietly and leave early, stopping to look back at her while telling myself not to fall for her. The air outside is already hot as I work through the city to begin the morning watch. I left a note left for Sara beside the bed to meet me later. I've told her nothing about my purpose in Florence, just that I have business I must attend to, meetings to take. She accepts the story, or seems to at least.

I'm barely to the café when I see Pippo and Scarlet come out of their building, overnight bags in hand, which for them could mean a week's worth of clothing. He's wearing his white shorts and loose fit button-down shirt, the sleeves rolled up, unbuttoned most of the way. It is his look for visiting the coast. Sea chic, he calls it. A car picks them up at the far end of the pedestrian street and disappears around the corner. If I had slept another ten minutes I would have missed seeing them leave.

My stomach turns. He recognized me that night

outside the restaurant. I know it. Our bodies had come in contact, faces inches away. How could he not? Is that why they're leaving? Because I'm here? But their bags are not for a long trip.

My stride is long, purposeful as I leave their street. My pulse races. I knew it would end in Positano since before I left Kansas. It had to. That's where it ended a year ago.

Sara is just waking as I come back through the door, surprised to see me.

"Did you finish early?" She crosses the room and wraps herself around me and I absorb her, allow her being to be part of me for that moment. It is one of the final seconds with her.

She retracts, retreats from holding me, my arms still suspended in the air where she had been, and her eyes cannot rise from the floor. I remain silent, unable to say anything. She forces her gaze up and as soon as it meets mine it falls again.

"You're leaving."

"I'm sorry."

She lets out a short laugh, a reaction to my apology, a defensive mechanism against the feelings we are both having.

"I know it hasn't been that long, Avery. But I like you."

"I like you, too." It is true. I can feel it, but have to hold myself back. I want to take her with me and walk beside the sea with her.

Sara is a diversion from my path, a distraction I gladly took. A complication I hadn't accounted for in months of planning, but one that is pleasant and magnetic.

"Are you coming back to Florence?"

"I don't know yet." I want to say yes, I am, and will find you and hold you until you are tired of me holding you, but I know I will likely be on a Lufthansa flight to New York.

Time away will be good, though. Distance is needed to regain my equilibrium, restore my balance and attention to the situation at hand. Each moment I stand here wanting to ask her to go with me is another step further away Pippo gets from me.

"When?"

"Noon train to Rome." I look at my watch and think of Pippo's gold Rolex. I caught a glimpse of it earlier, a reflection of light off the crystal, perhaps.

"One last stroll?" I say.

My bag is zipped up within minutes, what possessions I had remaining to be packed quickly getting stowed away. She stands near the door watching. It is the most uncomfortable I've been with her.

At the street her hand finds mine, where it fits perfectly. That was one thing Olivia didn't like, walking and holding hands. It had nothing to do with public displays of affection, just that she found it uncomfortable, always connected. She had no idea how couples could walk with the man's arm wrapped around his partner's body.

A small squeeze and a moment later she squeezes back.

Not much is said. I think we both just want the few extra minutes together. We stop at the end of the street that leads to the train station.

"I don't want to go any farther," she says.

I nod. She kisses me gently on the lips, her body maintaining a distance as she stretches to reach. My arms go around her and pull her in tight. Her hands reach up to my face and touch my skin as she looks at me fully, into my eyes, searching for something.

"I hope you find what you're looking for." Her tone implies knowledge of more than she can possibly know, that she has sensed something in my words or my moods.

"Thank you."

She turns and walks away.

The entire point of my trip is questioned as I watch her go. Every answer I needed, every accusation I have leveled in my mind. I am letting a wonderful woman walk away so I can chase a ghost.

She doesn't turn around to look before going out of sight around a corner.

CHAPTER FIFTEEN

Olivia and I overslept and scrambled around our apartment to grab what we thought we might need for a weekend at the sea. Neither of us had even packed swimsuits since we were staying in Florence the entire trip, so a stop at an overpriced boutique would have to be made on our arrival in Positano.

A black Mercedes van was waiting outside the building when we came out. The side door slid open to expose Pippo and Scarlet on the black leather seat. He held a glass of wine. Even for him, it seemed early for drinking.

"Are you coming?" Pippo said.

The van was in motion before the automated side door completely closed. Olivia and I took the second seat behind them as oversized vehicle worked its way through the narrow streets.

The mood in the van was dark. Pippo said nothing else and Scarlet sat on the other end of the bench seat from him, staring out the side window. It was a rare occurrence of the two not being in physical contact. I turned to Olivia to gauge her reaction but she was already leaning against the window, eyes closed.

It was minutes into the trip and I wanted it to be over. To just have the time with her we had planned. Days and nights roaming museums, drinking wine, and making love. Back in Kansas she rarely wanted to leave the house. We ordered dinner in or I cooked what few meals I could make. In Italy she wanted to be out constantly and make new friends.

The motion of the tall van around corners sent a swell through my stomach. I looked out the tinted glass to steady my horizon and saw us going through the stone arch at the edge of the city.

"Aren't we going to the train station?"

"No," Pippo said. "We are not." He was abrupt and for once short on words.

When Pippo didn't want to tell you something, he simply didn't tell you, but he was never quiet. He wanted to be the only one to know the whole story. He wanted to be in control. There was a level of acceptance you had to get to in order to spend time with him. I wouldn't say trust, as I never fully trusted him.

I watched highway signs through the early morning road trip, inhaling deeply through my nose, exhaling through my mouth, calming the motion sickness that was trying to fight its way out. Best I could tell we were headed west. After an hour we exited into the city of Livorno and stopped at the entrance to a private marina.

Growing up in Kansas I'd had few opportunities to go on boats. Small ones. Outboards, bass boats, and one ski boat at which I failed miserably, my face striking the water hard several times while trying to get the skis up on top of the surface where they should have been. I had never been on any body of water bigger than the Missouri River or the reservoir south of town. I'd stopped accepting invitations to go on boats when I finally realized I simply didn't enjoy it. My mother had made me learn how to swim when I was younger. My dad didn't care either way. I never saw him swim, or for that matter wearing anything less than jeans and a long sleeve work shirt with his name embroidered on it, or his one black suit that filled any other occasion that required clothing. We didn't go to the creeks or pool to swim as a family.

I followed them down the long dock bobbing on top of the water, no handrails or railings on either side. Olivia was in front of me and had no problem adjusting to the motion of the floating sidewalk, never losing a step. I stumbled once, more from nerves than balance. I'd have killed for a Dramamine.

A man dressed all in white stood beside a boat. A small yacht, I guess it could be called. There were two decks above water and portholes giving clues to a lower level. It was long and sleek. The hull was a shining white, everything above a brilliant stained brown wood. It looked old but perfect, the type of thing you'd expect to see a Kennedy or Cary Grant on.

We dropped our bags on the dock before boarding and walked across the gangplank with a thin white rope as a handrail. Following Pippo and Scarlet, we went through the first cabin then up top where a full spread of meats and cheeses awaited, along with more wine. Somewhere along the dock, Pippo's attitude had changed back to his more usual personality, the one that likes to be seen and heard.

"We eat, then we depart," Pippo said. "The skipper is still making the boat ready." He turned to look at the man in white with a hint of disdain, annoyed at being delayed.

The food was delicious, though did nothing to calm my stomach that had become upset at the thought of a long boat ride on the Tyrrhenian Sea. I drank more wine that I should have, my head feeling the effects of the alcohol before the boat left the dock.

The rumble of the twin engines vibrated the deck. Olivia stood and pulled me with her to the side to look out across the sea.

"Isn't it just perfect?"

"It is." I tried to hold back the nausea, to be there and strong beside her. I am a land mammal and was out of my element. The boat lurched forward and left away from the dock and I grabbed the railing, my knees momentarily giving way.

"Are you okay?"

"I'm just not really a boat person."

She put her arm through mine and took me inside. I stretched out on one of the long built in cushioned benches, the huge view of the sea only a foot above me through the window, but my eyes stayed away. Olivia sat with me for a few minutes, her hand stroking my hair. We were barely out of the harbor when I fell asleep.

A drunken sleep at sea is not a restful sleep. My mind worked overtime with the swelling motion of the boat, compensating for the movement, working it into dreams that made less sense than usual.

The sky was dark inside my dreams, but didn't feel like night. There were black, circling clouds blocking out any light while my body buffeted around in strong winds, searching for steps below me as the earth crumbled away quicker than I could move. I saw creatures ahead, three of them. They seemed large and dangerous, silhouetted though no sun shone to cast them into shadow. I couldn't stop moving forward, their shapes drawing closer with each step, but their size not increasing, until I was in front of them, their bodies still obscured. Two looked to be feline, but not like a domestic cat, and the other a muscular dog. I felt that beyond them was some place that couldn't easily be returned from, someplace darker, more dangerous.

The three sat on the last bit of ground which would allow me to move forward, and although not large or making moves toward me, I felt I could not pass.

The dream faded in and out, the sky always dark, until much later I found myself past the creatures, looking back at them, their backs to me.

"We're here." Olivia's voice woke me gently, allowing the dream to go away.

"Where?"

"Positano."

"Already?"

"It's been six hours. I just thought you'd like to see it from the water."

My legs felt steady, even as the boat rocked while slowing to align with the dock. My equilibrium adjusted to the constant motion. We went through the door to the bow where Pippo and Scarlet stood, ever present drinks in hand, his other hand on her ass.

"There you are," he said. "I know this is a much longer trip than taking the train, but there's nothing like arriving in Positano by sea for your first visit."

Pastel buildings spread from the water. A city carved into the mountain and painted in bright tones that had faded over the years to make the colors even more perfect. The sun was low in the sky behind us after the long boat ride, casting soft light onto the colors. The moment I took it all in I knew he was right that coming into this town by car or bus wouldn't be the same.

Shirtless men with sweaty skin and dirty pants stood on the dock and grabbed the ropes tossed to them by the skipper. Sinewy arms made quick circular motions with the rope around the iron cleats to secure us. The skipper was off the boat and waved down a boy with a makeshift luggage cart. Our small bags were placed on it and he pulled it away up the hill to Pippo's apartment, through the tourists working their way to the dock for the last ferry to Sorrento.

It was four minutes of frenetic energy, motion all around to end the long boat journey, then all was still again. The small city glowed above us while voices carried across the air from restaurants and bars.

With the day trippers mostly gone, the town was left to those staying in hotels and the few who lived there that came out to mingle with the people who could afford the vacation spot. I'd read about the nightlife in Positano, but we didn't make our way to those places. Instead a quiet dinner was had by the water with conversation far more relaxed than I was accustomed with Pippo.

CHAPTER SIXTEEN

When I woke, Olivia was standing naked at the window. Her body was a silhouette from the brightness outside, her shape unmistakable and perfect. I'd seen and touched those thighs a hundred times and never failed to enjoy it, whether clothed or naked.

"You look amazing," I said.

Her head turned, but not fully, so I could see only the line of her face, the hint of a smile.

"I want to live here," she said.

"In Positano?"

"In this moment, with you."

Her body came around and faced me.

"What would you like to do?" I said.

"Anything you wish, my love."

We had been tired from the trip and the wine and fell asleep quickly the night before, not taking the opportunity to be with each other our first night in Positano. I stood, naked from sleeping in the silk sheets, and went to her at the window. My hands reached her skin and took it in, slowly exploring every curve.

I turned her body toward the open window again, her hands going to either side of the frame as she leaned forward, her back arching, shoulders rolling back. I made love to her with the view of her in front of me, Positano and the sea beyond.

We collapsed onto the bed, sweaty skin against skin, and held each other. The breeze came through the window across us. I felt the effect on her skin from the cool against heat, the tiny bumps moved like waves, hairs stood on end.

"Why me?" I said.

"What do you mean?"

"You asked me once, so now I'm asking you. Why me, you and me?"

A pause before her response. "Why would you ask that?"

"I just wonder. I know I'm not a great catch. You can definitely do better than this." I motioned like Vanna White at my pale round belly.

"Shut up," she said. "You amaze me more every day."

I shook my head. "Nah. I'm just a boring guy with low self-esteem and a huge collection of old books."

She looked at me, her eyes focusing deep into mine. "You need to realize how great you are."

"But I—"

"No. You are. You treat me like no one ever has. You make me come like no one ever has. You look at me as if I'm the most beautiful thing on earth."

"You are."

"Hush. Your mind is brilliant but you won't accept that. You don't even see it."

"I write books for kids and teach college students things they'll never use again."

"Stop selling yourself short. I wouldn't be with you if you weren't a wonderful man. You create something from nothing, stringing words together. You grab the imagination of children, inspire them to read."

"You make it sound like so much more than it is."

She shook her head, resolving to lose her well fought argument, and retreated back into my arms.

"Why were you there?" I said.

"Where?"

"The book signing where we met," I paused, considering whether to tell her I'd seen her before. "And the event a few weeks earlier."

Her face went pink and she closed her eyes. "You saw me?"

"Third row back, fourth seat from the left."

She blushed more. "I can't believe you remember that."

"The rest of the audience was ten-year-old children who didn't want to be there and moms staring at their cellphones. But why you? I know you don't sit around reading *Kids On the Case* mysteries."

"I hadn't planned to sit. I was there shopping for a present for someone and heard you talking. I liked your voice."

"My voice?"

"Yeah. I liked your voice. Still do."

It was my turn to blush. "I've always thought I have a droning voice."

"No. It's sweet and sensitive sounding while also commanding. I just wanted to listen to you talk, so I sat down."

"Then again three weeks later?"

"Well…that one I planned. I looked you up. I may even have bought a couple of your books. Then I saw you were going to have another reading, so I decided to go listen again."

"Don't take this wrong," I said. My hand went to her face and stroked her cheek with my thumb. "But that's pretty pathetic."

She laughed loudly and grabbed a pillow, hitting me in the head with it. This turned into a wrestling match which turned into holding her for another hour.

The rest of the day was spent wandering the hilly streets, looking in small shops, and eating lunch with a view of the sea. I bought her a bikini that left nothing to the imagination and a pair of trunks for me that were far more form fitting than I preferred, but finding anything not skin tight is difficult in Italy.

With the swimsuits obtained, she wanted to get into the clear water immediately. We changed in the shop and wore them to the public beach beside the dock. There was no sand, only rocks that made it difficult to walk. I watched as children and adults, browned by the daily dose of sun, strolled barefoot without a wince. I limped along, stopping and swearing out loud at the pain against my soles, my thoughts on the overpriced sandals back at the boutique and how I would have worn them right into the water had they been purchased.

The water was perfect and once away from the beach, feet afloat in the surf, it was calm and comforting. Though nervous about being in the sea, even surrounded by so many people, I floated along with her.

Each minute in the water gave me more confidence until I was floating well away from the rocky shore, my head leaned back until only the sky was in my field of vision. I could still hear people laughing and having fun not far away but my body was weightless, feeling more as if the water were pushing me up rather than my weight forcing me deeper. I closed my eyes. Water formed a ring around my face, the rest of my head submerged, the muted vibrations of splashes and voices traveled beneath the surface.

It was the most comfortable I had ever been in water. Maybe it was having Olivia near me, or perhaps just the added buoyancy of the light level of salt in the sea, but once in, I didn't want to get out. We floated for what seemed like hours as the world moved around us.

We met up with Pippo and Scarlet late in the evening at a restaurant he'd given us the address to, and dined and drank as the cool sea air flowed in with the magnificent sunset over the mountain. Boats left white trails on the water far below us, fading as the light turned to dusk and then dark with a dramatic display of orange and red in between. Each second in this place was a new view, a new masterpiece that lasted only moments before being replaced by another.

Pippo and Scarlet had been drinking before dinner and were already in their party mood before we connected with them. A third bottle of wine was ordered once our meals were finished and plates taken away.

"This place is more than I could have imagined," I said. "It's magical."

Pippo leaned back in his chair and pulled from his wine glass. The ocean was behind him, his white shirt framed perfectly with the black around him.

"If Florence is the heart of Italy," Pippo said. "Positano is the vulva."

I choked on the wine I'd been sipping. When I saw his serious expression, I stifled the laugh that had worked its way out, turning it into a cough that was believed by no one.

Pippo poured the last of the wine, splitting it between Olivia and my glasses.

"In Florence you soak in the art, the spirit and history of the country. You drink great wine to enjoy the flavor of the grapes grown outside your door. And you make beautiful love."

"Then what do you do in Positano?" I said.

"In Positano you drink cheap wine to get drunk. You mock the tourists. And you fuck."

He reached into his pocket and pulled out a small silver case I hadn't seen before. It was opened and four pink pills fell into his palm. He placed one in Scarlet's eagerly outstretched hand before putting one in each of ours.

I stared at the pill. The edges were jagged and the outline of a coiled snake was engraved on it. Though nothing was said, I knew what it was.

CHAPTER SEVENTEEN

Colors emanated from everything as the beauty of Positano soaked my skin, oozed through my pores and gave me new life. Every time I touched Olivia I thought I could feel her heartbeat as if it were my own, two bodies connected, conjoined, one. She had become light, a beacon to pull me in as a moth fluttering around her brightness, her flame.

Shoeless on the rocky beach, running and chasing each other with no regard for the stones. No pain or sadness, no thoughts of tomorrow or home or anything beyond right then. Only love and sexuality released, opened like a hose on a summer day as the drug continued its coarse through my veins.

In dark water, still clothed, material floated around our bodies, white shadows swayed and swirled around us. Olivia's dress orbited her, swelling in and out with the current, as if a great jellyfish had surrounded her.

Deeper into cooling water. My feet could touch,

Olivia's couldn't. She swam to me and her legs wrapped around my waist while we kissed, hints of salt from the sea on our lips. The water was calmer than during the day, no boats pulling in constantly at the dock, sending wakes into the swimming area. Sounds from the city still floated down the mountain, through the narrow lanes, to the ocean that gave Positano its life, the fleets of fishermen long gone.

The initial shock of the cool water at night had gone away, now replaced by the comfort of it supporting our bodies, holding us up, moving us against our will.

She looked into my eyes and I felt her affection for me, her love, and I knew she could feel mine. Everything moved slowly, bobbing and circling as the water controlled our motion. Our bodies stayed near, closer and further with the tide, touching, releasing, then touching again, as water splashed between our chests.

I heard a gasp, a sound I had heard Scarlet make a couple nights earlier. The small bit of moon in the sky caught their skin and I saw them entwined in the shallows, his body atop hers with water moving across them. His back was bare, a shirt left somewhere on the rocky beach, and shone with the wetness of the sea water, muscles tight in his slight frame, flexed like an animal preparing to kill.

Olivia's hand moved down and felt me and it was only moments before we, too, were making love in the water. Every touch, every sensation, was heightened. My heart pounded fast, the drumming sound vibrated my temples. I wanted as much of my body as possible to be in contact with hers, to be inside her, to move as one with her, to become one with her. As hands moved and mouths explored necks I felt our anatomies merge, skin grew together until we were one mass in the water. Above us the stars were bright, spectacular impartial voyeurs to our actions. They cared not what happened down below.

The beast I imagined we had become writhed in the sea, contorting in its new life form, an animal created out of lust that consumed raw emotion to sustain itself. We understood and fed it as much as we could, moving faster and accepting our new existence, one whose only purpose was to reach rapture in the pleasure of the flesh, while being one with the earth and sea, to release adrenaline and endorphins at rates never experienced by a human.

We had moved through the water. I don't know if we floated or swum or found another level of being to travel from one place to another, but as my hand came around Olivia's body, I felt skin across the back of my arm. Without a thought, without hesitation, without consent, my hand turned and took in this new body with my fingers, as soft and smooth as Olivia's.

Scarlet.

We were beside them, the thin strip of water between us violent with the motion of four bodies. While looking Olivia in the eyes, I ran my hand across Scarlet's flat stomach and took hold of her breast, fingers taking everything in. Pippo was on his knees, holding Scarlet's hips to his, her legs wrapped around his waist as he continued to thrust inside her. Scarlet's hand went to Olivia's face, caressing her skin, down her neck, stroking her breasts as Olivia finished, as I did moments later. My hand still on Scarlet, Olivia's went to Pippo's arm, fingernails digging into olive skin. His motions became more intense. Scarlet's moans grew louder until she startled the night with her final orgasmic breath.

We left the water holding each other, laughing like we were two couples who'd just climbed off a ferris wheel at the county fair. The climb through the town was effortless as feet felt light and floated across the ground. Scarlet danced in the narrow, winding streets to music only she could hear and Pippo joined her, trying his best to keep up with the tempo that altered at her will, his chest still bare as his shirt floated out to sea in the rippling currents.

I watched Scarlet as she moved. Her wet dress clutched her, exposing every nuance of her shape. Her dark skin shone through the white cotton and as she spun, arms raised in a dance she invented right in front of us, I could see the small pink circles on her breasts and I wanted to feel them again, to taste her lips.

"I want to kiss you, Scarlet."

I heard the voice as if it weren't my own, reflected off the faded pastel walls of the village above the shops and restaurants. It had come back like a song and I wondered if I'd sung the words.

In constant motion, twirling and dancing, Scarlet orbited me, going around my body and Olivia's as if not to separate us, until she stopped in front of me. Her hands came to my face and her mouth came to mine. We touched and I felt the heat from her body so close and tasted the wine she'd been drinking and the salty sweat of Pippo left on her lips. Then she was gone again, spinning into the darkness as the tempo changed once more.

Emotions were fluid as I felt my lust for Scarlet and my love for Olivia, and somewhere in there an acceptance of Pippo, an admiration, an attraction of sorts that I couldn't understand. I looked to my left and saw Olivia smiling at me.

When we arrived at the apartment, wine was poured as it always was, and music was turned on loudly, finally allowing the rest of us to hear what Scarlet did. Her dance continued as she floated through the room, her voice magical as she sang with the melodies and created her own that somehow merged with the music and became something new, something wonderfully beautiful. I watched her dance without shame, taking in her body with each turn, each move of her hand across her face, her chest. Her wet dress was removed, leaving her naked as she continued her performance.

Olivia was beside me. I don't know how long she was there, watching me as I watched Scarlet. She reached up and kissed me on the cheek, the neck, as her hand worked its way downward, traveling between the material and my skin. The moment her hand touched me, my body trembled as I became firm. I fought my desire to watch Scarlet and turned to Olivia, who smiled at me while shaking her head slowly, and gently turned my head back to the other woman.

The room blurred, Scarlet the only thing in focus as she saw us, Olivia's hand moving inside my slacks, and she smiled. Scarlet floated toward us until her hands were on my chest. There was a moment, a look between the two women, as Olivia touched Scarlet's bare shoulder and brought the other woman's body to mine, giving me to her and her to me. Olivia's hand came off me as Scarlet's lips touched mine. This time mouths parted and tongues met.

As if planned, timed to the precision of an atom splitting, we took each other in, hands glided across bodies, my clothes were removed. Never slowing down, she moved me to a seat and brought her leg over me, paused for a moment to look at me, gaze touched gaze, and she lowered herself on top of me.

I felt her surround me as I had dreamt over the last week. How I'd craved her. Naked I saw her fully before me as I had when she'd been with her usual lover, but this time she was mine. The effect she had on a man, to make him feel he is the only one, was exaggerated, increased in magnitude.

My eyes were connected to her, taking in every curve, every motion, from closer than I'd ever been to her, from inside her. I inhaled her scent, tasted her skin. From the nothingness that existed outside of us, the penumbra of reality ever darkening as my hunger for Scarlet was being satisfied while also growing it, enabling it to become stronger. A flash in my periphery, something that pulled my vision, my attention.

I glanced, taking my eyes from Scarlet for the briefest time possible, not wanting to be separated from her in any way. As I looked back to her, in her eyes I saw a refraction of what I'd seen, a splintered version through light and shadow of bodies connected, hands pushing down, fingers around a neck, as Olivia lay beneath Pippo across the room being controlled, restrained, fucked.

CHAPTER EIGHTEEN

Voices on the street below came through the open windows, entering my subconscious and infecting my early morning dreams while my body fought for more rest. Faces formed and melted with no details available as fragments of conversations from different voices tried to piece themselves together.

Buongiorno! … pulisci il marciapiede … non dare da mangiare al gatto …

I raised my hand to my forehead. Shockwaves of pain flared through my body. Everything hurt. My tongue was dry and my head ached. My eyes open for the first time and blinked to the brightness of the room, struggling to see.

The pill.

Had I taken it? My mind raced, trying to put each second together. Dinner. More wine. Then I recalled the moment the small pink pill was placed in my palm, the rush of adrenaline I'd felt, the sudden fear of being ridiculed for rejecting it like high school peer pressure to drink a beer stolen from someone's father's garage refrigerator.

But I hadn't rejected it. Looking at Olivia and her mischievous smile I had placed it on my tongue. I held it there too long before washing it down with wine. The bitterness, the synthetic taste of something so unnatural.

The dark water. Swimming with Olivia in the beauty of the sliver of moon off her skin, reflected in her eyes as we'd kissed.

And Scarlet.

I tried to sit up quickly, but my body didn't allow it and I stayed horizontal. *What had I done?* Then the act came back to me, my hands reached out in front of my face as I remembered them on Scarlet's perfect body, stroking her skin, feeling her on me. My eyes tightened as if to cry, but nothing could come out, no tears were left, no moisture in my body.

Olivia came out of the bathroom and jumped on top of me.

"Fuck!" The pain was immense, every muscle seemed in contraction simultaneously.

"Get up, sleepy head!"

My head wouldn't move from the pillow. I managed to open my eyes again to see her dressed and looking as beautiful as ever. The sight made me forget my pain and I raised my head, wanting to tell her, to apologize, to try to explain what I had no explanation for. I stopped, head barely off of the pillow, with a long grunt.

"I thought so." She reached to the bedside table and brought back a glass of water and three pills. More pills.

I looked at them in her hand.

"It's just Tylenol, silly."

She helped me sit up and I took the pain relievers and drank the whole glass of water. I needed to confess my sins, to come clean about the night before. My incomplete story fighting to come out.

"I'm very—"

"Dehydrated. Yeah. I know. You needed to be drinking water last night instead of the three bottles of wine you had."

"Three?"

"Three."

"Damn."

"And from what I can tell, they were about $500 each."

"Wow. Wish I remembered them." I took her in, fresh and peppy, ready for the day. She was so happy and I couldn't say what I needed to. "How are you so awake?"

She shrugged her cutest shrug and leaned in to kiss me until she smelled my breath.

"You, to the bathroom, now." She climbed off the bed and pointed. I obeyed. "Shower and get dressed. Swimsuit and a light shirt."

"Why?"

"You'll see."

"I just want to sleep."

"Now!"

The bathroom in our suite was larger than the apartment we'd rented in Florence, with a walk-in shower big enough for a party. The hot water felt good against my skin and not being crammed in against tile walls felt better. I took my time even though she walked in every two minutes to check on me.

I closed my eyes and let the water run across my face. More thoughts of the night before. My pulse sped up and I got hot, turning the water cooler to compensate as I began to sweat in the shower. I remembered the sex with Scarlet, being with her more than once, in ways I had never experienced before.

A fear hit me that Olivia would leave me, but as her name floated into my thoughts, so did the memory of her giving me to Scarlet, offering me to her, a smile on her face. And of seeing her with Pippo, him naked, holding her down, her legs on his shoulders. I remembered him looking over at me and Scarlet while fucking my girlfriend as I fucked his. There was no other way to describe it. There were no acts of love and it transcended mere sex. There was an aggression to it.

In a reverse of emotions so sudden I became angry at him, saddened by her, and it passed quickly with the realization of what had occurred. The drugs. The wine. I thought of Olivia telling me a few days earlier that she didn't mind me looking at Scarlet and wondered if it had all been something she'd wanted, even planned. She wouldn't…

When I came out of our suite, Scarlet and Olivia were waiting for me. Nothing was different from any other morning. Nobody seemed concerned about the events that had taken place. I had to pause to think about my memory, to validate it. A glance around the room and I see the chaise lounge I had reclined on, Scarlet on top of me. My shorts I'd worn the night before were still on the floor beside it.

Scarlet caught my eye with a grin and I swear a wink so subtle it could easily be written off as a trick of light and shadow.

On my way to the door I glanced left into the other suite. Pippo was standing in front of his open suitcase, a worn leather binder in his hand while he scribbled with a pencil.

Scarlet yelled from outside. "Come on, Pippo! We're supposed to be there already."

He didn't look up as he continued to stare at the book, scanning whatever was written on the page.

"I'm coming now." He looked at the Rolex on his wrist.

As Olivia stepped back in to grab me, I saw Pippo put the binder in his suitcase, covering it with neatly folded clothes.

Outside I forced a smile at Olivia. "Where are we going?"

"You'll see."

CHAPTER NINETEEN

There is always a life to the Tyrrhenian Sea. A surge. Never is it calm enough to reflect the perfect blue skies. It defies the serenity of the coast, the perfect and composed towns where people go to relax and offer themselves to the sun, as if in intentional juxtaposition. Chaos and calm.

With the engine off, the boat rolled side to side, forward and backward, in a constant mimicking of the water. At speed, the salty spray arced over the hull onto whomever was there to receive the blessing from below.

The boat was much smaller than the one we'd ridden down on from Livorno. There was no cabin, only a small deck in front of the skipper and a bench seat behind him. Olivia made me walk the narrow access to the front and lie down with her on the padded surface, leaning against the small bridge. Pippo and Scarlet took up residence on the seat in back, bodies connected in as many points as possible, one leg over his, her arm draped across his back.

Any hesitation I'd had about riding on boats seemed to have disappeared. I don't know if the long ride from Livorno had reset my inner ear or the relaxing air of the Amalfi Coast had me not caring. The boat moved along the coast to our right where homes older than I could imagine hung off cliffs over the sea. It is impossible to look at them and not wonder about living there, leaving everything behind in Overland Park, Kansas, and sitting at a desk overlooking the ocean everyday, typing out the silly children's mysteries that brought in far more income than my professor duties. Perhaps even write the great novel I had always wanted to before getting sidetracked with tales of three children looking for clues about lost milk money, only to find out the school bully had taken it. The school bully was almost always the culprit, the children's mysteries equivalent of the butler.

Olivia in my arms on the sea under the Italian sun was all I could ask for. It was a moment I wanted to hold on to and remember whenever I needed it, in those moments I was away from her, when back in the classroom with blank faces staring at me, uninterested in learning about Faulkner at 8 a.m. on a Tuesday. The splash of salty water was refreshing as we heated up, unprotected from the sun, the canopy only shading the couple behind us.

The coastline on our right drifted away as the boat continued straight, not turning with the land to wrap around toward Sorrento. I sat up to get a better look over the elevated bow as it continued its off-beat rhythm of smashing down into the water. The rocky mound was still miles away but I knew what it was. I turned to Olivia.

"Capri?"

She smiled.

We had talked about it when planning the trip, but had decided to stay north in Tuscany to explore the arts she so loved. We figured there would always be time for another trip. Things turned out different, but not unwelcome. What trips I'd taken in my life were within whatever radius the family car could take us in a day of driving, usually returning the next day due to my parents needing to get back to work. To be on a private boat headed to one of the most beautiful and expensive islands on earth was a culture shock, to say the least.

We drew near the island and the boat slowed as I took in the rocky walls that grew straight out of the ocean, up into the air. For most of the island, there are very few places to get ashore without climbing the face of a cliff or scrambling over huge, sharp stones. It isn't like the sandy-shored isles of the South Pacific, approachable from any direction, unending beaches to run on, sleep on.

I heard Pippo behind us say something to Vincent, our skipper. The boat slowed more and turned into a cove, stopping a dozen feet away from the wall. Vincent stepped past us to the front with ease on the rolling boat and lowered the anchor.

A loud splash came from behind the boat. I got up, holding onto the railing for support, just in time to see Scarlet in a thin red bikini jump into the water. Pippo was already in, floating on his back.

"Yes!" Olivia scampered to the back of the boat and had her shirt and shorts off before I could catch up with her. She stepped down to the platform beside the motor and dove in.

"Come in, Avery!" Pippo said.

I was down to my form-fitted swim trunks, looking at the rough water. I could see the rocks at the bottom and turned to the skipper.

"How deep is it?"

He looked over the side with a shrug. "Twenty-five meters, maybe thirty."

"Right." Eighty-five feet of clear water. Possibly deeper.

"Do not worry," Vincent said. "Is almost impossible to drown. The water is too salty."

"That's not the most comforting way to phrase that."

Olivia called for me. I looked at her and only her and jumped.

I was submerged, my eyes defied me and opened, taking in the blurred view underwater. For the few moments I was beneath the surface, I saw the rocks below and a school of tiny fish swim past me, unfazed by my presence. The soreness from the events the night before were pulled from my skin, my muscles, while suspended in time, weightless. I'd never liked swimming, avoiding the city pool when I was young. I probably haven't been fully underwater in twenty years. Now I wanted to be down here all the time, just from the seconds before returning for air.

My head broke the surface with no effort from me, my body floated easily in the salty water. Olivia was beside me. Her hand touched my chest under the water. Mine felt hers.

"Over here," Pippo yelled. He and Scarlet were moving away from us toward the cliff.

Swimming in the rough water was not easy. The surf fought back with every inexperienced stroke. It felt like an effect from a horror film, the hallway stretching out ahead of the young woman as she ran from a crazed killer, never able to reach the end. We caught up to them feet from the opening of a cave. The entry was only a few feet tall and no wider than that as well.

"You must see inside. Hurry, we don't have long!" Pippo was not a man who waited for answers or approvals, he just knew people would follow. It was his personality, part of the reason I liked him and at the same time the entire reason I detested him.

I reached the mouth of the cave. The water swelled up and down, striking the rock on either side of the opening with such force it created a loud clapping sound. One by one I watched them swim in, moving right down the middle, the current still sending them side to side, as they adjusted with every stroke to keep from hitting the walls. Enough light reflected in from beneath that every submerged stone was visible, distorted by the water to look perilously close to bodies swimming past.

Facing fears was never my strong point. I avoided whatever scared me my entire life. To this day I can barely ride a bicycle. I didn't fly in a plane until I was thirty, opting to drive wherever I needed to go.

My heart raced more than just what was needed for the physical exertion of treading water. In reality, that wasn't even much. Vincent was right. The high levels of salt in the sea made bodies very buoyant. I could lean back, spread my arms, and float for an hour if I wanted, as I had in Positano.

The bobbing heads were barely visible in the dark corridor by the time I made my entry, light from the outside world lost to the grey stone surrounding them. I had never suffered from claustrophobia, but entering that cave made my pulse pound. The first few feet were the hardest, where the water was at its most volatile. It remained rough, but was far more manageable without the swells pushing my body side to side. I couldn't turn back to see the entry. I don't know if I was more afraid of seeing how far away the opening was or that perhaps the open sky and water was just behind me, no great distance traveled.

It grew calmer the farther in I went. The miniature whitecaps were gone, just the undulation of the water rising and falling. It was too dark to see the bottom, and I don't know if I wanted to. What you can't see in the water is what is most daunting.

Voices. I could hear them, could pick out the different tones of Pippo's booming bass and Olivia's high-pitched laugh.

By the time I saw the light I was in the cavern. They were almost motionless in the middle and I thought they must be standing on a rock hidden underwater. When I reached them I understood why they were so still but not how it was possible. The water moved around our bodies, circular, coming from below us in a contained riptide that instead of pulling swimmers to sea, kept explorers afloat with little effort. It was at the same time exhilarating and unsettling, feeling the force of the earth, the effect of the moon on the tides, the slow process of water eroding stone to create a subterranean oasis that only the bravest, and myself, would ever see.

The light from the tunnel we came down was gone, blocked by the slightest curve that I hadn't even noticed while entering. But we were bathed in crystalline light. It came from below us in an optical illusion not easy to solve. I stared down through the shimmering water, eight legs moved in time in slow circles to stay in place more than to keep afloat in some otherworld synchronized swimming demonstration. Nothing below produced the light. I looked up to see the smallest hole in the rocks. It was perhaps five inches across and shined with the brightness of a kitchen light in the middle of the night.

I thought of the boat ride and what time we'd left Positano, and realized it was near noon, the sun at its highest point it would be that day. I had seen the cliff we anchored beside. It was taller than the water was deep, ten stories at least. This hole had to be straight through, no curves or bends or the light wouldn't travel as it did. How many years of water drops would it take to create such a natural phenomenon?

The four of us floated, suspended by the light from above like marionettes doing the sun's bidding, bodies glowing from the beams reflected below. Our voices echoed and we all talked softer, not needing the loudness. The real world seemed far away. Unlike a traveler to the moon, where it would take three days to return home, we had only to swim a few minutes to break into the sunlight again.

Then Scarlet began to sing. The sound amplified, reflected off the rocks around us. It was a song I did not know and that made it sweeter, more magical. The words and melody would be associated with this place, this moment, and no other. No one else spoke or interrupted her or sang along. We all stayed silent in our weightlessness, listening to her voice surround and envelop us. The final notes came from her as the brilliance began to fade from the earth's continual rotation. The sunlight striking the opening way above us was off center and darkness was coming fast, along with the silence, the song now over.

The blackness overtook the cavern more quickly than I was prepared for.

"We need to go," I said, trying to mask the desperation in my voice.

A laugh from Pippo. "Not yet. This is the best part."

I looked over at Olivia who was oddly calm in what I could see of her face in the quickly diminishing light.

The reflection below us dimmed as sun from the natural overhead fixture was moving fast away from its direct path from above to below.

"Everybody look to the exit," Pippo said. "Know where it is but do not move until I say."

I wanted to go then, make my sprint through the water while there was still a hint of something to see.

Then it was gone. The light from above no longer cast itself down into the water and the reflection went to black. Legs formed wide circles beneath the surface as they had been, but I couldn't see them. I couldn't see anything. The absence of light tightened in on me, compressed my chest. I inhaled hard through my nose to attempt regulating it, controlling the intake and output of oxygen and carbon dioxide. I was failing.

"It is time! Follow me." Pippo's voice joked in the dark as splashes of arms through water echoed. A hand glanced past my shoulder then returned, holding me gently for a moment.

"You okay?" Olivia spoke softly as if to keep the others from hearing.

"Yeah," I lied.

"I'll lead you there."

"Can you see?"

"No, but I can hear them. Keep your hand on me and listen to the water beside you. Let it guide you." She was so calm it soothed me enough to move and follow her.

The sounds of clapping against stone grew louder as we moved and her words made sense. I moved left when it grew too loud on my right, small movements within the narrow channel. My heart still pounded but I felt a regularity to it, a solidity that was comforting. It motivated me. Moved me along.

Complete blackness. Without any light to see the walls, to see how small the tunnel was, the sense of claustrophobia went away. My hand came off her back in the new sensation, the new strength. I kept my arms stretched out to my sides, not wanting to strike the wall and risk hitting my head.

"You back there?" Olivia's voice pulled me.

"I am."

My left foot brushed something hard and soft at the same time, firmness behind silky smooth, a stone below the water covered in what grows in such places, I hoped. I adjusted right, ears alert to the sounds, the echoes.

A brief silhouette ahead of me, Olivia's head bobbing, moving, then it came again, sharper in detail. We were swimming through the curve in the tunnel and light was forcing its way to us once more.

It came on quickly after that to where it was blinding after the time in darkness. Once I broke through the entrance into open water my eyes were adjusted. Away from the cliff I turned and looked at the opening. It seemed larger to me now, easier to manage than it had when we first swam through.

I could hear Pippo laughing behind me, then Olivia was at my side, looking back at the cave with me. Her hands greeted my body and we swam out into the open water together. Once clear of the rocks we tread water, face to face, and I looked her in the eyes. She kissed me and stayed there until we got back on the boat.

Vincent worked the steering wheel and throttle, moving

us forward and backward with no progress for several minutes while the four of us sat in the back of the boat taking a respite from the sun until we were underway and had to distribute our weight more equally in the small craft.

"The anchor is stuck," Vincent said. "I have to go in to see so I can free it." He pulled his shirt off to reveal his light brown skin from day after day of being on a boat. Then he lowered his black shorts and let them drop to the ground revealing bright green Calvin Klein briefs. "I hope you don't mind. I have no extra clothes with me."

Shrugs and nods were given, not concerned with what he had to do. We were lined up on the wide bench seat, bodies relaxing and dripping with salt water with Vincent still in front of us, still not in the water to free the anchor.

His thumbs went into the waistband of the underwear and with a startled movement I turned my head away, the closest thing to offering him privacy on the small boat, while wondering why he had to strip further. I saw the other three still looking forward, then all eyes grow wider, including Pippo. I turned to look as Vincent stood naked in front of us, unashamed and with no reason to be.

I can say I had never been that close to another man's naked body in my entire life without any hesitation. What videos I'd searched for online in times of physical need rarely included men. Olivia's arm across my back tightened on my shoulder.

Vincent walked naked to the bow of the boat, looked down into the water, then took a small step forward and disappeared vertically into the sea.

CHAPTER TWENTY

I began the trip not caring if I looked like a tourist, or more accurately, not knowing the difference. I chose to bring comfortable clothes for walking around in the heat, nothing too fancy for dressing up. Olivia didn't try to dress me, but she always looked perfect in her lightweight sun dresses or perfectly fitting shorts and camisole tops.

Vincent pulled us up alongside a private dock for a waterside restaurant where two men held the boat steady and gave hands to step over. The maitre d' met us there and we followed him up to the building with a large open patio where splashes of water from the sea curved up toward the guests before arcing away in a display designed to make your expensive dining experience just that much better.

We ate and drank for two hours. Glancing around I wondered if, or which, of the other guests came from the big yachts we had passed, the ones with their own helipads and miniature submarines. We were all eating the same shrimp entrees and drinking the same bottles of wine, but the similarities ended there. I would reach for the check when it came but it would be taken care of by Pippo without even an acknowledgement of my effort. I still had to try.

It was another world for me. A normal day for Pippo and Scarlet. A weekend at home might see an outing to a neighborhood chain restaurant, or perhaps into downtown Kansas City for something a bit nicer. For the likes of Pippo, taking a private boat to Capri for lunch was normal.

A white convertible taxi, a minivan with the roof cut off, one of the few cars on the island, drove us up to the town of Capri where upscale boutiques lined the winding walkways selling clothes I could never afford. The island is a high-end shopping mall at sea.

We ate gelato and walked more, stopping at every opening to look out over the water. The white wakes of boats far below us stretched and dissipated into the surf. We saw the yachts anchored off the island, contrasted by boats smaller than the one we'd come over on that had nothing more than a wooden bench seat and a motor you steered with a handle, right is left, left is right. The working-class transportation of Capri.

The town is all hills and we grew tired of walking, taking seats at one of the overlooks. Even Pippo seemed to gaze out across the world in awe though he'd seen that sight a thousand times. I looked at Olivia and occasionally at

Scarlet and saw men attached to other women look in their direction.

"We have some business to tend to tomorrow." Pippo broke the silence. "But I've arranged for Vincent to take you to Amalfi, or wherever else you choose."

"That's too kind, you don't have—"

"It is done."

He made it hard to dislike him, as much as I wanted to. The times he was loud and obnoxious were almost made up for by his generosity. Of course, it wasn't his money he spent. His family subsidized his lifestyle but I had no reason to judge him for that, being the benefactor of his good grace.

We rode down to the marina and Vincent took us back out to sea. He asked if we wished to stop for another swim. Pippo gave him directions and the boat sped off.

Anchored again at the far end of the island, the mainland not visible and only the open ocean to our left, the cliffs were more amazing than any we'd seen. Pippo stood on the bow looking up at the shear rocks, his eyes working their way from the waterline up to the top.

"This will do," he said.

He was down to his swimsuit again and nothing else. In a smooth motion, he dove off the side of the boat, his arms rising out of the water in endless strokes that propelled him toward the island.

"What's he doing?" I said.

"Showing off." Scarlet chuckled as she said it, always amused by her man's actions. "Let's swim."

I pulled my shirt off and turned to see Scarlet and Olivia's naked bodies jumping into the water. A glance to my left at Vincent who watched them indifferently, a sight he'd seen often.

"You like your job, I guess?" I said.

"I do." He nodded.

"Are you from here?"

"Born in Sorrento and still live there."

"You speak English very well, you know."

"I like American women, so I practice to speak to them."

"Have you ever been to America?"

He gave a smile that had probably opened a thousand pairs of legs. "America comes to me." His eyes were still on the women in the water.

Olivia motioned for me to come to them. In defiance of the manhood I had seen from Vincent the skipper earlier in the day, I pulled my swimsuit off, stepped down to the platform at the back of the boat, and jumped in. They were floating beside each other and turned to face me as I stopped in front of them, very aware that the clear water hid nothing below the surface as I saw their incredible bodies and knew they could see mine.

As I put my hand around Olivia's back in the warm water, one of Scarlet's hands came to my chest, the other to Olivia's shoulder. We treaded water, holding each other, not speaking. Hands moved beneath the surface and across naked skin until I wasn't sure whose hands were whose. I grew excited as they each kissed me, starting with my shoulders, then my neck, then my mouth, alternating as we kept each other afloat. I went from one pair of lips to the other, tongues mixed with salty water. Hands worked me, back and forth, slowly, tightly. It was difficult to remember to kick my legs at times, to stay above water, to care about taking in air, as the two beautiful women touched me. I wanted to feel both of them, give them the pleasure I was receiving while surrounded by water, but could tell this moment was for me, whether they'd planned it yesterday or in the moments before I swam up to them or it had happened with no intention. Both of them had hands on me as I finished, our eyes connected as I kissed them each again. They stayed with me, hands still on skin, lips on lips, aiding in my buoyancy until I was able to breathe normally again.

A voice echoed and caught my ear. We had floated farther from the boat and turned so I was facing it. Vincent stood on the bow watching us.

It was probably the third time Pippo had yelled that our attention was taken off each other. Scarlet looked over my shoulder and grinned.

"He's a lunatic," she said.

I didn't want to let go of the moment or their bodies, but I did. Turning, I scanned the water and didn't see Pippo.

"Where is he?"

"Up there," Olivia said.

I glanced to see her hand pointing up, followed her direction, and found him. His arms were stretched as far as they could go, one above him, one to the side, as his feet searched for purchase on the rocky wall. He was forty feet off the water and still climbing.

"What the hell?" I said.

"He loves doing this," Scarlet said.

"Doing what? Trying to kill himself?"

Pippo had reached a ledge almost halfway up the white stone cliff. He turned and sat on the narrow rock and waved his arms at us to make certain he had his audience. More smoothly than I thought possible in the small space, he got to his feet, toes over the lip of the rock. His arms stretched out to his sides as he straightened his back, legs together.

"He's not—"

"Oh, he is," Scarlet said.

"Is the water deep enough?"

"Maybe," she said. "Maybe not."

I looked at her then back up at the cliff where Pippo stood, arms wide, as if Jesus Christ himself were about to take flight. His knees dipped, body arched and dove forward, and Pippo was soaring through the air. The fall felt eternal as we watched his toned body, arms and legs tight together as he became a projectile, a missile headed straight for earth with nothing to slow it.

My breath was held. Scarlet laughed behind me. I imagined a hundred outcomes in the seconds he was airborne.

He broke the plane of the water with little splashing and from our distance, no noise. It was as if he had disappeared, one minute a human existing on this earth, the next gone. Seconds went by, then more. I imagined him below the surface, his body limp after striking a rock he hadn't seen before climbing, blood spreading through the waves. Then a small splash and Pippo's baritone yell echoed off the cliff he'd jumped from.

"He's really going to die doing that one day," Scarlet said.

Olivia and I rode in the back and let them take the front area. I enjoyed the shade of the canopy and relaxed into her body. My arm pulled her in tighter. As my finger stroked her shoulder, I thought of the night before, of being with Scarlet and seeing Olivia with Pippo. I wanted to be outraged at her and at myself, and especially at him, but I wasn't. I couldn't be. I was a part of this now, complicit in all actions. I wondered briefly what it meant for me and Olivia, our lives when we returned home. Would a generic two-story home in the heartland be enough for her? Would it be enough for me?

Pippo had said that sex in Florence was the most pleasing. Animalistic. Maybe he's right, but that is true about all of this country. One can't think of Italy without fantasizing of romance and love and sex. It's a different culture than the center of America. Perhaps bodies are meant to be more free than I was taught through sermons and Sunday school. Perhaps love isn't digital, only on or off for one person, but analog. The wires and circuits that created the purest sound of an old record player through a tube amplifier compared to the compressed and rigid digital signals from computers. Maybe emotions are meant to flow more freely, more openly, with more people, like harmonics widening the note to include more than what we think we are hearing, what our ears are capable of taking in.

My parents married young, right out of high school, and have been together ever since. Only a few times in those years have they been apart for more than a night. I don't think either ever cheated or even thought of being with another person. I never caught them having sex or even heard anything that made me think they were being intimate. Perhaps commitment to her faith keeps her from enjoying the flesh. This is my role model, for better or worse. Complete devotion to each other and to the Lord. Since moving out for college my attention to church had waned significantly but I never was unfaithful to a romantic partner. This was different. My partner was beside me, supporting me. Watching me.

The boat slowed enough that the water wasn't crashing over the bow, wetting us all. I thought nothing of it, just that Vincent wanted a more soothing ride for us. Capri was far behind and we still had a way to go before paralleling the mainland coast.

I was leaned back in the corner of the boat to see around the bridge to the view ahead. I saw the two pairs of feet off to the side rather than legs stretched out toward the bow. Then it dawned on me that they were facing opposite directions. Pippo's hand came into view, pushing out to the right, Scarlet's hand trapped beneath his as his body arched up. I leaned my head over to see better. His clothes were off as were hers. He was moving on top of her fast, aggressively. Even over the motor beside us and the hull against the sea, I heard her let out a gasp, one I knew well from having been inside her.

"Are they?" Olivia said.

"They are."

She grinned then nodded her head. I followed her look. Vincent was standing in front of us steering the boat. One foot was up on a shelf under the wheel as his left hand was inside his shorts stroking as he watched Pippo and Scarlet have sex.

More than America comes to him.

CHAPTER TWENTY-ONE

"Scarlet suggested we stay in Positano a few more days." Olivia tossed her hair over her shoulder as she said it, knowing that always distracted me, and made me more agreeable to anything.

We sat at a table below the grand steps to the *Duomo di Amalfi*, the beautiful cathedral that had presided over the small town since the 10th century. The square was full of tourists taking photographs and buying ceramic tiles with picturesque scenes of life along the Amalfi Coast painted on them.

"We're supposed to go back to Florence in the morning," I said. "We have an apartment there. The rest of our clothes."

"But this place is just so…" she stopped talking and looked around at the town, hoping it would finish her sentence for her. When it didn't, she continued, "I think we should stay. I want to."

"I just want to be alone with you," I said. "The two of us."

"Aren't you having fun? We're traveling around Italy without spending a dime. We're staying in a luxury apartment in Positano, taking private boat trips, eating incredible food." She paused and brought her hand to my chest. "Having incredible sex."

There was no way I could explain without sounding petty. It was all too much for me. My life was good back home. I made enough money, more than most, and could afford what I wanted. But being here, being with them, it made me want more. Pippo had never worked a day in his life. He partied and drank and fucked and woke up to do it all over again, no regard for what people who don't come from a wealthy family do. He met a girl he liked and took her into his world of decadence. He took whatever he wanted.

And being around him, I wanted to, also.

I had experienced a fraction of his world, his life. We'd seen Florence and Positano in a way I'd never have been able to on my own. I told myself I wanted to go back to Kansas, to my small world, but only because I knew I couldn't have his life. He wasn't going to take us in as he'd taken Scarlet away from her life as a shop girl, selling dildos to tourists in Amsterdam. It wasn't sustainable and far from practical.

I tasted a different world, a different existence, a different woman. I wanted to be with Olivia, yes, but was captivated by this other way to live, to have a person I loved and still enjoy others as well. Floating in the sea with Olivia and Scarlet, touching each other, had been a turning point, an acceptance of this other life that I hadn't fully given in to out of fear. My guilt for having sex with Scarlet had gone away. My anger at Pippo for being with Olivia disappeared. I loved Olivia and she loved me. I knew that. And now I knew that there could be more to that love. Each night we could fall asleep together, alone, or with someone else, and everything would be normal in the morning. Or some decadent form of normal.

That wasn't a viable solution for someone working a full time job, living a normal life in the suburbs. It was for people who travel when they want, drink when they want, and have sex when and with whom they want. That was Pippo. He had lived it for years and had indoctrinated Scarlet into that world. I was standing on the doorstep looking in, enjoying the fruits of his lifestyle while still being outside.

I wanted it all. The money. The glamour. The sex. Even the drugs. When I thought about my home in Kansas, it had become claustrophobic. The house, the job, the modest German luxury sedan that had been my only splurge from the money I made writing children's books, the rest sequestered to high-yield investment and savings accounts.

Still she sat there, looking at me. It was a pivotal moment. A line in the sand. If I said yes, I felt it would be near impossible to ever go back. And if I said no...I didn't know. Would I be returning to Kansas alone?

I didn't ask her for fear of the answer.

My mind spun, looking at both paths, trying to look

into the future of what they held. Perhaps I could stay, enjoy the gluttony, and still go back. Maybe we can come back often, every summer, and pick up where we left off each time, an adult Narnia full of carnal desires. I scrambled for an answer, a way to ensure it, a way to keep Olivia no matter what.

San Gimignano. The rain had struck our skin as we stood there that day, our bodies merging into one with the passing storm, and that day I had known. None of the events of the last few days changed the way I felt about her, what I wanted with her.

I turned to Olivia with the answer, which came in the form of a question.

Her face was blank. I couldn't tell at first if she was shocked or upset. I felt like I was back under the water, waiting to surface while at the same time not wanting to.

"What did you say?" She was shaking her head slowly as if in disbelief, confused. I feared it was the answer but asked her the question again.

"Will you marry me?" The second time it came out as a request, a statement. Something Pippo would say, offhanded like "Let's order more wine," no upward lilt at the end to signify requesting permission, but rather an order.

Her mouth opened and closed several times, words formed then dissolved as her expression changed in the seconds that passed, until a smile formed on her mouth, then she was on me, the chair pushed back into a man drinking cappuccino at the next table.

CHAPTER TWENTY-TWO

It felt incomplete. Not real. It wasn't romantic. It was logical. I loved her, and I wanted to be with her. My proposal was not premeditated. If it had been I would certainly already have had a ring at the ready. I still fall back to the traditional things. *Would she take my last name?* I wanted to find a jewelry shop right there in Amalfi, to buy her the best ring I could, to be official, to feel complete. She wanted to wait until we returned to Florence. It was the heart of Italy, she reminded me, and the place that meant the most to her.

We walked and held hands still sticky from lemon sorbetto. I kissed her whenever I could. At the top of the grand steps to the cathedral I held her tight, my arms around her from behind so we could both look out across the city.

"I love you."

She turned and kissed me. "I love you, too."

"You can be happy with me?"

"I already am."

"In Kansas?"

"Wherever you are. Wherever we are." Her head leaned back against my chest. "Can we come back to Italy again?"

"Of course we can."

The important days never stand out as such. I hadn't awakened that morning feeling something special would happen. At bedtime nothing would be different. We'd brush our teeth and crawl under the sheets. Perhaps we'd make love. No matter what else happened on the trip, we were together.

But it was important. We would go to bed and wake up the next morning something else. The question was asked and answered. In a way it is already done. In our minds we are together. Betrothed, as they say. The parts to come later are ceremonial. Legal. From that point she said "Yes" we were officially together, not just boyfriend and girlfriend. And still the day felt normal. I liked that about it. No fanfare. Maybe we should just do it while here. Get married in Florence in a few days. My mother would be pissed if it weren't in her church with her pastor, but in time she'd get over it. With grandchildren she'd get over it.

Scarlet screamed and ran across the room, grabbing Olivia and hugging her so tight they both fell onto the sofa. Pippo looked at me and nodded his approval.

"This means we celebrate," he said.

I didn't know what a celebration night looked like compared to a normal night so I was excited and a little nervous.

"We will have a party," Pippo said. "Tomorrow night. Tonight, we get drunk."

And we did. We started at a restaurant on the water and within minutes of arriving the liquor was flowing. Food was an afterthought. As usual I never had to open my wallet. The drinks just kept coming.

We moved from club to club, always starting again with bottles that emptied quickly. Others move in and out of our group as they did when Pippo was partying. We danced to loud, obnoxious music. I moved from Olivia's lips to Scarlet's freely, hands explored their bodies in the cover of the crowd.

Exhaustion from drinking and dancing taking over us, we took the walk back up the hill. The mood was more subdued.

"You will get married in America?" Pippo said.

I glanced at Olivia. "Yeah. Most likely." I hadn't yet brought up the idea of doing it before we headed home.

She smiled and nodded.

"We will come, then."

"To Kansas?" I said. The thought of Pippo in Overland Park was frightening. He'd scare the locals and I wasn't sure the state had enough wine to appease him.

"That would be so incredible!" Olivia said.

"Maybe we come to one of these book readings of yours."

"I really don't think you'd enjoy that."

I relaxed on the couch as more wine was poured into my still half full glass. My eyes struggled to stay open in a state of exhaustion and drunkenness. The song changed and Olivia jumped up, arms raised, with a scream of delight and began dancing. Scarlet joined her.

I hadn't thought of teaching or writing in days. The real world was a blur, a history that almost didn't seem possible. My home, my car, paying bills, it was all a distant memory.

Drifting in and out of sleep I watched them, smiling. Olivia and Scarlet were euphoric in drink and dance. Sometimes it felt like they had known each other far longer than the couple weeks it had been. There was a quality to their relationship I couldn't place. It wasn't sisterly or best friends. It was almost a deeper connection than that. A bond.

Eyes closed, music faded, then opened again.

A different song was playing. Slower, a little quieter. I don't know how long I'd been out. Minutes. An hour. They held hands, fingers interlocking with arms raised between them, gyrating to the beat. Laughter.

Out again. Silence. Calm. Then a rush of images of Olivia and me, together. A vision, perhaps, of what was to come. The life we would have, but I couldn't place where we were. All around us was in smooth bokeh, the perfect blur of the background in a photograph, obscuring the location, focusing on only us. But we were together and happy.

I stirred. Olivia's hands were on Scarlet's hips as they slow danced to an old song that sounded of cellos and a woman's voice that was telling a story of love and sadness in words I couldn't understand. A glass was still in my hand, unspilled through my intermittent lapses of consciousness, and I managed a sip of the wine.

Scarlet's hand went to Olivia's face, tracing her outlines with a fingertip, down her nose, across her upper lip.

Olivia's hands pulled and Scarlet's body moved in as their mouths touched, lightly at first. Then they kissed, heads tilted and tongues moved around each other, as hands roamed across bodies, under clothing.

My eyes strained to stay open. To see. As Olivia pulled the narrow straps of Scarlet's dress off her shoulders, nothing on beneath the material, her perfect and smooth brown skin exposed, my body gave out and I slept.

CHAPTER TWENTY-THREE

The water splashed against the wall beneath me, sending salty sprays across my bare feet and legs. The first ferries were coming in with loads of tourists to canvas the small town in search of the perfect souvenir for themselves, their friends back home, or to appease the coworkers who always expect a token from each person's vacation.

I woke earlier on the edge of our bed with barely any sheets covering me. I rolled over to see Olivia asleep with Scarlet behind her, arms wrapped around her. Raising the sheet, I saw their naked bodies. My imagination didn't have to work hard to figure out what had happened. I only wished I could have stayed awake to take part, or to just watch.

From the shower I could see them still, asleep and peaceful, as I washed myself. Part of me wanted them to wake, to see me there, wet and covered with soap, and join me in the shower. Another part of me wanted to disappear, to get away from what had been happening, to recover and become who I once was, where waking with two beautiful naked women wasn't normal. I appreciated the experiences, don't get me wrong. They are the thing of teenage and college fantasies, that when they don't happen by a certain point in your life you accept that they aren't going to. Once the more uninhibited and explorative days of college end or you approach your thirties and the expectancy to find someone and settle down bears on you, the fantasies remain just that, not something you think might happen late at night after a wild party at an off-campus house.

I gave in to staying a few more days in Positano. The proposal was how I found a way to remain and still be able to leave, to go back to my small-town life with a chance of surviving. I'd be going back with her. I hadn't even had time to think about the drive to Wichita to meet my parents or the holiday party at the college president's house with her at my side, heads turning to see her attached to me. I could love her and want to show her off, too.

With shorts, a loose-fitting button-down shirt, and sandals, I walked down the hill to the sea. Over the days in Positano I had seen the town close its doors for the night and wandered the streets while it slumbered. As the lights turned off and lanes turned to shadows from uncovered porch lights, it took on the feeling of an older time. The buildings were hundreds of years old, or more. Walking through Positano late at night was time travel to when things were simpler.

This was my first time seeing the town wake for the day. Shop owners swept and hosed down the sidewalks in front of their stores while cafés brought in fresh boxes of produce or placed pastries straight from the oven into display cases. The smell of sugar and cappuccino occupied the air.

I struggled to remember what day it was. We'd left Florence on Friday. Had it been three days in Positano? Four? Did it matter? Most lives are spent in service of a calendar. When you go from living that existence, knowing what you'll be doing on Thursday afternoon three weeks from now, to one where you can't recall what day of the week or month it is, you get an unsettling state of confusion. At first each day there is a sense of not being where you are supposed to be. What meeting are you missing? What bills need to be paid? Then even that goes away, replaced with only the here and now. The days spent in service to the sun and the sea, the evenings honoring Bacchus by drinking the wine that came from the soil of Italy.

I'd stopped carrying my phone when the battery died and I didn't bother recharging it. I hadn't checked email in a week. My wristwatch was tucked inside a pocket of my suitcase back in Florence. Time was gauged by day and night, broad strokes rather than minutes or hours.

Pippo wore his Rolex every day, but for him it was a status symbol rather than having any need to be somewhere at a certain time. I hadn't seen him without it, even swimming in the sea or when he dove off the cliff.

He told us it had been a graduation present from his father when he finished at the University of Turin and he hadn't gone a day without wearing it since.

Another ferry docked and unloaded to my left with the rush of tourists eager to explore an ancient village in the morning, another in the afternoon, then be back in their hotel restaurant in Sorrento for dinner. A family walked past me, the parents holding their children's hands until clear of the scramble of tennis-shoed and sandeled passengers off the boat. The father had on a Kansas City Royals T-shirt. Maybe I sat near them at a game once. Maybe the children would recognize me from my photo on the backs of my books. Probably not. I couldn't keep from staring at them, taking in their motions, their moods. It was like looking back through the wardrobe into the real world. The mother was talking quickly to the kids, who were maybe nine and eleven years old, giving them instructions on how to act and not to wander off. She'd probably given them the same speech at every stop. It was a family vacation spent in frustration and worry rather than relaxation. The dad was already looking at the ferry ticket booth signs to see departure times and comparing those to the clock on his phone.

I didn't want to be like that, and hoped I hadn't been during our first days in Florence. I followed Olivia blindly, let her be my tour guide. Seeing the family in front of me was a flashback to childhood, being ushered around Six Flags in St. Louis for eight hours until we had to drive back home, eating sandwiches carried in with us to avoid the overpriced fried food sold in the park. Thoughts of work flashed through my head. Leaving home to be in class on time or at a faculty meeting. My agent had been hounding me before the trip for the next book's outline, a step in the process required by the publisher to earn my advance on sales, an amount that would more than pay for this trip. Olivia had pulled enough from my investment account to pay for the airfare and apartment rental as well as spending money. There was still plenty left, but I enjoyed the satisfying feeling of opening my quarterly royalty statements from my publisher and transferring the automatic deposits over into the higher yield accounts. It was more than a safety net at that point. It was a comfortable retirement wherever I wanted.

The water sprayed up on my feet again and everything else slipped away. I let the thoughts go and enjoyed the cool morning air. I was amazed at how easily I'd learned to do that. Let it all go.

"Hey, you."

It didn't register at first that the voice was directed at me, with all the people around. I was thinking about finding a cappuccino somewhere. And a croissant, maybe.

"Avery."

I turned. Olivia was there, leaning on the wall beside me, close enough I should have smelled the soft floral scented lotions she spreads on her skin before ever hearing her voice.

"Hi." I smiled as I said it. I always smiled when I saw her. I looked around. "You're alone?"

"Yup. We've been kicked out of the apartment for the day."

"Oh?"

"Party preparations."

I looked back out at the water. "Right. The party."

"Second thoughts?"

"About you, no. About the party, yes. But I also know we have no say in the matter."

"You're right about that. I heard Pippo on the phone with a caterer when I left."

"A caterer?" I shook my head and watched the swells move toward me from a ferry backing in, the next in an endless stream of them. "Maybe I misjudged him."

"What was that?" She poked me with her finger. "You misjudged him?"

I smiled. "A bit. He's still a bit…much, but he means well."

Her arms went around me and she kissed my ear.

"What should we do today?" she said.

"I'm thinking first a cappuccino and a croissant, then a quiet day together getting lost."

"I like the sound of that." She was looking past me with a grin. "Come with me. Hurry."

I grabbed my sandals and ran behind her barefooted. The ferry that came in had just finished unloading and the two crew members were standing behind it facing away. Olivia ran across the gangplank into the cabin and I followed. We climbed the steep stairs to the upper deck and sat in the front row of seats, sliding down to keep from being seen from the dock.

"What are we doing?"

"I figured we could get cappuccino somewhere else."

"Where's this ferry going?"

"I have no idea."

We covered our mouths to keep from being loud with laughter. When passengers boarded, we sat up and pretended we belonged. They never checked tickets once you were on.

The ferry powered out into the sea. The air was still cool and I put my arm around her, neither of us prepared for the wind away from shore.

"Which way will it be?" she said. "Left is Amalfi. Right is Sorrento."

The boat kept a straight line until a hundred yards out before committing to a direction, Positano still looming beautifully before us. We angled starboard.

"Sorrento!" People around us looked at us like we were crazy.

It was a smoother ride than the small boat a few days earlier but still bumpy. At least we were well above the spray of water. Paralleling the coast, we watched the same houses clinging to cliffs we'd seen the other day.

"Which one?" I said.

"Which one what?"

"Which should we live in?"

Her finger went to her mouth, tapping her lower lip in deep sarcastic thought before pointing. "That one looks nice."

"I like it." I motioned to another. "I like the peach colored one."

"It's small. Couldn't entertain."

"You're right."

We'd reached the end of the peninsula and turned right to stay along the coast. A brilliant white house seemed suspended in air, nothing but trees below it, the cliff it was balanced on obscured by greenery.

I glanced over my shoulder then back at the house and pointed.

"That one."

"Why?"

"It has a view of Capri."

She sat up and looked left. The rock stuck out of the sea five miles away. The morning mist blurred the sharp lines we'd swam beneath.

"It's perfect."

Daydreaming with Olivia was magical but I couldn't tell how much I was joking around and how much was what I really wanted to do.

Sorrento sprawled for miles compared to the smaller towns on the Amalfi Coast. It was home base for most tourists, with every ferry starting and ending there and a train station to connect to Naples and farther. We climbed the winding road and steps to the town high above the water to the city's square and stopped at a café to finally have our morning cappuccino.

Once done and walking around the town again, I found it comfortable, more approachable. It didn't have the posturing that Capri or even Positano did. Shops were affordable and clerks friendly to everyone who came in. Every other storefront had tables of huge lemons, the local specialty.

"I like it here," I said.

"Why's that?"

I glanced around. "I feel like it is people more like me."

"What are people like you like?"

"You should know."

"I'm interested to know what you think you're like."

I thought about it. It had been a feeling, nothing I'd formed into words yet.

"People from small cities and towns, like me. People who work hard five days a week, take their kids to soccer practice in minivans, and plan family vacations two years out."

"Is that who you are?"

"Not all of it, not yet at least, but yeah."

She was quiet, taking in the people around us.

"I grew up in Manhattan, you know," she said. "Didn't move away until I went to Kansas for work. Never planned to stay there long. Always thought about going to the west coast."

"I've been thinking about that." I stopped in front of another shop with huge lemons and picked one up. It was heavier than I expected. "I can move somewhere else."

"Oh, right. Leave your parents and your job?"

I shrugged. "I see my parents every few months as it is and could get a job teaching anywhere. I can also support us on just my books." She doesn't know the extent of my writing income, that I could quit the college job and never look back as long as I kept churning out the *Kids on the Case* books and parents kept buying them.

Each year new kids age into them and discover all twenty-three volumes and counting and I see my royalties surge with every Scholastic flyer handed out in third and fourth grade classrooms around the country.

"You've really thought about this."

"I have."

"You don't have to support us. I hope to work in a museum someday."

"That's a load off because I really don't want to work any harder." I laughed and she gave me a soft push.

The afternoon grew hot and she found a lemon grove in the middle of town that served fresh sorbetto and limoncello. We got two frozen cups and sat under the trees.

"What time are we supposed to be back?" I said.

"Scarlet just said tonight. Which for her could mean anywhere between seven o'clock and four in the morning."

"This is true."

"It'll be fun."

"I'm sure it will. And it will be over the top and crazy and who knows what will happen."

CHAPTER TWENTY-FOUR

The sun sets late in Italy in the summer, so it was still high as we boarded a ferry. The next one departing went to Capri before Positano. After paying for our return tickets, we got our front row seats on the top level again and settled in, my arm around her, head on my shoulder.

As we approached Capri, a line formed in the aisle beside us as people took turns to get to the front to take photos with cameras and phones. "You haven't taken any pictures," she said.

"Don't need to." The island was large to our left as we slowed. "I won't forget any of this, and the only person I'd want to show the photos to is here with me."

"You're cheesy."

"That shouldn't be new information."

"It is not."

We docked on the far side of the island from where Vincent had dropped us off for lunch and our exploration of the town. A few people got off, but being late in the day, we mostly took on more passengers headed back for the night.

The air was cooling off again, bookending our day together. A layer of clouds hung just above Positano when we arrived, below the tops of the mountains surrounding the town, making it feel like a dream, a vision one only had late at night when thinking of faraway places. Lights were coming on in advance of the sunset still a couple hours away. Glowing strings outlined restaurant patios as people in colorful clothes wandered the paths around the pastel buildings.

We walked up the hill to the apartment, taking our time before the craziness commenced. I hadn't wanted to avoid it, but just wanted more time with Olivia. That was what I missed most about spending so much time with Pippo and Scarlet, was time alone with Olivia. I loved the quiet times with her. The nights spent curled up on my living room floor talking for hours. Mornings sleeping late as suburban sounds found their way through double paned glass; lawn mowers firing up, children playing, and neighbors talking over the tops of wooden fences.

I pause before opening the door to the apartment. A moment of silence before the night ahead. In the main room a long table of food was set up with two bored looking servers standing idle in the corner staring at their phones. A note from Scarlet on the coffee table said they would be back soon and to get dressed for the "night of our lives."

I was exhausted already.

"I'm going to take a shower," I said.

"I'll join you."

"I was hoping you'd say that."

I washed her body and she washed mine. It was slow and sensual, relaxing and caring. We kissed and held each other as the hot water crossed our skin. I believe we both felt it was a time for something else, something romantic, a few moments together alone before we weren't.

Olivia put on a black dress I hadn't seen before that made me look forward to taking it off of her. It followed every line of her body. I watched it slide down over her freshly lotioned skin, the scent filling my nose and acting like an aphrodisiac. She chose my clothes from a selection left by our hosts since all of ours were still in Florence. A pair of linen pants and a light pink button down with the tails out. Standing in the mirror I looked at myself and liked what I saw. I ran my hands across my stomach and could tell there was less there, that some of the mass was gone.

She saw me. "You've lost weight."

"I have?"

"Yeah. Noticed the other night."

I smiled at her and she kissed me. As I put my arm around her to kiss her again and perhaps take the dress off her earlier than planned, the front door slammed shut and Pippo's booming voice echoed through the apartment.

"Where are you? It is time to celebrate!"

We stopped, faces an inch apart, my lips craving to touch hers again. "Shit."

"Stop it," she said.

"I know, I know. I'll enjoy myself. Then later, I'll enjoy you."

"I hope that's a promise."

There will be time to kiss her later. And tomorrow. And the day after that, as we begin our lives as something more than just two people.

She put her hand on my cheek and looked at my face, moving her eyes to take all of me in. I felt exposed, open to her. Anything I tried to hide, she would see. In her eyes was something new, something I didn't recognize. A new feature to her beauty, or another layer I hadn't yet been allowed to see until now. I couldn't tell.

"What?" I said.

"Nothing. I just wanted to see you for a moment."

"You're sweet."

"Just remember, no matter what happens, it is you I love and want to be with forever." A tone to her voice that wasn't familiar. Melancholy. A sadness.

"Me too," I said.

She left the room and I watched her go, the black dress clinging perfectly to her. No matter what happens, I thought.

Guests arrived in a constant flow of faces I'd never seen. Most acted as if Pippo was their oldest friend with screams of delight at seeing him and Scarlet. One of the servers was tending the bar and had trouble keeping up with the demand for drinks. Music played loudly and voices were even louder, mostly Italian and all excited.

Sometime into the party the apartment was at maximum capacity and spilled out onto the balcony. I lost sight of Olivia occasionally when she'd go to get more drinks. I was grateful that no announcements were made and wondered how many people even knew the reason for the celebration. Pippo didn't screech the music to a halt and tell everyone, give an inappropriate toast. A few people did congratulate me, but most, it seemed, were just there for a party no matter the occasion.

I looked around the room at tanned faces and bodies as the wardrobe for the evening seemed to require as much skin showing as possible. Men's shirts were unbuttoned. Women's dresses were cut low at top, high at bottom. It was the rich and beautiful of Positano surrounding me, a children's book author from Kansas. As I scanned, something clicked and I looked again. A face registered as familiar, but everyone was in motion, talking and eating, kissing and dancing, and I couldn't find it again.

Conversations were short due to lack of interest or language barriers, which was fine with me. I kept personal details to a minimum and looked at Olivia whenever I could, and Scarlet when I couldn't.

The crowd thinned after many hours and when the food and drink supply dwindled.

"Make sure you run out of alcohol at the right time," Pippo had told me, his arm across my shoulder, his signature musk filling my nose. "That's how you weed out the crowd."

Soon, only a dozen or so people were left and I saw the familiar face again. I turned to Olivia.

"Is that the boat skipper?"

She looked where I was motioning without pointing.

"Looks like him. Vincent, right?"

"Right."

Scarlet stepped into our view and pulled us to a corner of the room, a devious grin on her face. She looked amazing, as always. Her dress hung loose on her body but clung to skin in just the right places. She wore no bra and from experience I knew probably no panties, either.

Scarlet held her hand out to us. "Something special for tonight," she said. "Pippo called in a favor for these."

The two pills were baby blue with the outline of a butterfly on them. They were a little bigger than the last ones but similar. The edges were rough, not like the smoothly rounded mass-produced pharmaceuticals we'd buy back home.

"Is it stronger?" I said.

"Don't be scared." Scarlet placed a pill on the tip of her tongue then stepped to me, reaching her head up to mine. I opened my mouth and took her in, the pill transferred to my tongue, then lingered as she kissed me.

She then put another on her tongue and kissed Olivia the same if not more passionately. Her hands went to Olivia's sides, her breasts, before separating.

"What about you?" I said.

She handed me one more. I reached up and took her hair behind her head in my hand and pulled it tightly. Her body went rigid. I held the pill between my fingers just out of reach of her tongue. She moved forward for it and I held her back with my grip on her hair. She released a gasp. Olivia's hands were on my arm and chest, supporting me, caressing me, enabling me. Scarlet reached again and I let her tongue take hold of the blue pill as I pushed it into her mouth with my fingers. She closed her lips and sucked on my thumb as I pulled it out slowly.

I released her hair and Scarlet took a half step back, her eyes on me in stunned silence before smiling.

"Later," she said. "You. Me."

I gave the slightest nod and she walked away.

Olivia kissed me then stared into my eyes with a smirk. "Who are you?"

She pulled me to the area where people were dancing and began her slithering motions. It was difficult to watch her and move my body at the same time, but she'd take my hand and turn me, rub against me. We drank from glasses of wine that never ran out, deep red Italians that warmed me from the inside. I felt the drunk come on fast but didn't know if it was that or the pill. I hadn't eaten much during the party after our day in Sorrento snacking on whatever we found that looked good.

Songs changed, speeding up and slowing down with each new track. I knew some of them but had never heard most. My body became loose, fluid. Hands felt separate from my arms when I'd raise them. I could smell Olivia's perfume, her lotion, her skin. We were a single unit dancing, a creature again that couldn't be separated.

A few others were still there. Some sat on the sofa looking stoned, others danced near us, with us, around us. Pippo and Scarlet were in our orbit and at times our arms and hands joined them to us. I kissed Olivia. I kissed Scarlet. My hands took in their breasts, between their legs, slowly stroking with my finger, only thin material separating us.

Faces and bodies flowed from focused to blurred and back, the room swirled with brilliant colors. The voices were all beautiful, some singing along with the music, others just talking, laughing. It created new notes and arranged chords never heard before. A streak of heat went through my body, beginning in my toes and escaping through my eyes.

Scarlet's hands were on my chest as my head leaned back, shoulder moving in circular motions, and I think I was singing as I reached a new level of high, one different from the last time. I felt like I was glowing.

"There it is," she said.

I smiled at her and kissed her hard, taking her tongue into my mouth as I pulled her dress up and felt her with my fingers, caressing, penetrating, with no regard for who remained in the room. She tensed as her back arched.

Another hand moved across my shoulder, down my back. It was bigger, stronger. My tongue connected with Scarlet's again as the strong hand reached around to my front and felt me aroused. I'd turned my head to see Pippo kissing Olivia, a hand on her breast, his other on my crotch, fingers wrapping around me through the linen. A moment of confusion. I looked down and back at him, letting signals pass to grasp what was happening. My body defied my preferences and remained aroused at the foreign touch.

My hand flew down on top of his to stop him, holding it from moving any more. As a quartet we froze in unison, my fingers still inside Scarlet with Pippo's hand gripping my cock. I had to work to hold still as everything around us was still moving. We were trapped in the middle of a carousel out of control, the background muddy and changing shapes while we became marble.

I thought of the statue from Florence, the miniature replica on the shelf in his apartment. The Rape of the Sabine Women. Petrified figures in ecstasy or agony, I was never sure. It was Pippo's favorite. We were conjoined as they were, bodies paralyzed.

Olivia's hand came to my face and turned me to her. She said nothing but looked at me. It was wordless, a motionless request in her eyes. A release. A request. I wasn't sure. We held like that for what seemed eternity, all at my will, awaiting my response.

My thoughts jumped, landing on one memory then another in rapid fire. That wasn't who I was, what I did. I'd never laid hands on a man or hoped one would on me. It wasn't something deep seeded from Sunday school or sermons, it was just preference. Who I loved, what I liked, what excited me, was feminine. The smooth skin of Olivia and inherent seduction of Scarlet. The scared and gentle touch of my first true love in college and the unavoidable pain I'd caused before she had found pleasure, her never having experienced sex before that night in a darkened dorm room to shade her shape in naive and embarrassed humility, and me with only a few spite fucks in the back of a Mustang as the one to take her innocence. The thoughts of the cheerleader's hand first touching me and the shiver that had taken over my body. The newness, the excitement of it. A feeling that could never be felt a second time, the first touch from your first lover, even if not in love. It was a feeling you remember deep inside of you, coveted and cherished and wishful that you could feel it again though you know you can't. Olivia had described that late at night after she'd been with Scarlet, a second chance at a first feeling. She had found that, different but the same. An excitement. A taboo lifted, erased when you accept bodies and people, ignoring genders and norms and angry sermons that threatened damnation. The fear reduced to hesitation, that moment on the edge of the high dive that you accept you are going to jump, you just don't know when, with the sensation that a thousand eyes are on you, waiting, anticipating, judging.

Olivia's eyes were still locked to mine. My field of vision narrowed to only her, the rest of the room disappearing.

"This is what you wanted, remember? To experience something for the first time again. To feel that excitement."

My eyes never left Olivia's as my hand came off of Pippo's. As it had suspended, the motion begun again, four bodies evolving together. Hands moved freely from person to person. I kissed one, then the other, met Pippo's eyes with mine, then my lips with his.

Darkness and light alternate, strobing. Moments. Hours. Seconds. A zoetrope, stop action flashes in my eyes. Hands, lips, breasts. Mouths on bodies I didn't recognize and looking down to see a stranger on mine. Hair pulled, teeth drawing blood. Tongues exploring, swirling, tasting, taking in everything around. Faces appeared and went away, replaced, erased. Scents, odors, stinks. Hands on skin, hair. Feeling. Fucking. Bodies were interchangeable, preferences were fluid, moving from person to person. Wetness and friction, moans and gasps.

My mind gave in to the drink, the drugs, the emotion, the night. I was farther from home than I'd ever been, further from my childhood, my innocence. Faces came and went. Olivia. Pippo. Scarlet. Vincent. Some I had never seen before that night, nameless in our entwined limbs and broadened sexuality. I experienced pleasures I'd never known and gave them to others.

As vision cleared, focused, I saw only Olivia. My love, my reason. The things I'd experienced thanks to her, due to her, because of her, were a part of me now, never to be taken away or forgotten, whether I wanted to or not. My periphery sharpened as the drugs diluted further in my blood, decreasing the effects from a hallucinogenic half-life.

Never did I try to leave or say no. The look in her eyes hours earlier asked me to accept, told me to enjoy, to experience. And I did. Faces and limbs thinned as revelers faded to the side, leaving or passing out, or opting to be with only one person to end their night, until I was with Oliva, alone, in our bed.

Our eyes locked as I was on top of her, in her, as the room continued its spiraling around us. It was the terminal release of the night, the morning, and we came together, deep breaths and fingernails drawing deep as we finished.

She looked at me after, perhaps still more under the effects than I, her body nearly half the weight of mine. In her eyes I could see how she cared about me. Affection in hazel rings. But still as before the party there was something else. Fear? I rolled to her side, my arm going around her, and curled her body into mine. She shook.

"Are you okay?" I said. "Are you crying?"

She didn't answer but I could feel the moisture where her face had been buried in my chest. A hand clutched my arm as if trying to keep from falling, spiraling. I held her as tightly as I could as she came down from the drug.

I wanted to make her better, happy. Slowly her body relaxed and I let mine do the same.

In restless sleep I dreamt that night. Shapes turned to buildings, large stone formations around me. I recognized the outline as the *Piazza della Signoria* in Florence, though crudely drawn as if from blunt pencils from a child's memory. As I tried to walk, walls crumbled, disappearing into the ground, shaking violently. I was left in a field at night as I had been with Olivia what felt like months ago.

The stars above were bright as they had been with her. I saw the Great Bear in the northwest and Pisces just over the horizon. I walked toward it, never gaining ground, until Aries began to appear as the inky black grew lighter in hues of burnt orange.

I opened my eyes to our darkened room. The silence in the apartment felt foreign after the party. The music and laughter was gone. I could feel the weight of Olivia's body beside me in bed and sat up slowly to not disturb her. My head was thick and threatened a headache.

My equilibrium forced me to take a step forward when I stood up. Fluids weren't working as they should, still under the effects of the drugs, I thought. A pair of underwear were on the floor but I knew picking them up and getting them on would be difficult, so I left the bedroom naked.

The main room was void of people but the signs of the party were still spread everywhere. Empty wine and liquor bottles dotted tables and the floor. I paused to look at the large sofa and thought briefly about what had taken place there, arms and legs and genitalia connecting, in flashes of memories fighting to come through while I also tried to subdue them, not ready to remember.

I took four Tylenol with a glass of water in the kitchen and washed them down. A look to my right to see the door to Pippo and Scarlet's suite closed. Perhaps more than just the two of them in there. For a moment I wished Scarlet would come out, as naked as I was. Just the thought aroused me.

As if I willed it, the darkness changed, a low creak sounded as the door opened then closed again after Scarlet stepped through. She turned and saw me, her brilliant black skin reflecting what little light was allowed into the room from the open windows.

"I thought I heard you out here," she said. Her voice should have felt foreign in the moment, a collision of sound and vision in the vacuum, but was soft and blended with the dark. It felt as if I was still in the dream.

I moved left into the main room and she paralleled me in the hallway until we were in front of each other. She stood motionless, so close that skin should be touching but wasn't, her hands at her sides. I knew what she wanted. When I'd fed her the pill hours earlier as I controlled her. The look in her eye then told me she liked it and though I'd never held a woman like that, I liked it, too.

My hand came around to her hair and took hold, firm, solid, forceful. She exhaled quickly. I brought her face up to mine, her feet stretched to remain on solid ground as my lips approached hers but didn't touch, hovering. Teasing. I took her neck with my other hand, her own weight choking her, breath strained, gasping.

My mouth to her ear. "Is this what you want?"

A weak sound came from her. "Yes."

I moved toward the sofa, her toes working to keep up, to offer some support, until the backs of her legs touched the soft material and bent. Releasing her neck, I took her right arm and twisted her, turned her away from me, forcing against her joint and bending her over in front of me, her arm locked behind her. I felt the tension, ligaments and tendons stretched to their limits, ready to give, to tear.

Her knees went forward onto the edge of the sofa as I took myself in my hand, harder than I'd ever felt, and forced myself inside. She gasped as her fascia stretched to allow me in. I thrust hard, feeling her tight around me, bringing me close to climax fast as I pulled her long hair to stretch her head back. Her hand moved to touch herself, and I felt her shake as she did. I reached around and grabbed her neck and pulled her body up, forcing her rectum to tighten around me more, while holding her throat to block air, to restrict her breathing as she came with me.

I released her arm and she stayed in her position for a moment before standing up. She turned to me, eyes connecting with mine. I leaned in and kissed her, taking her lower lip in my teeth. Her fingernails went into my chest as I bit down and broke skin and she released one final whimper.

Letting her go, I stepped back, turned, and went back to my room, leaving her in the dark, feeling like a different person than I had been before.

I went into the bathroom and relieve myself, then wash my hands while looking in the mirror. Even in the shadows I could see the difference, more than just weight lost, but muscle tone formed. And beyond that, something undefinable. A variance in my appearance though I was obviously still me. Almost imperceptible. Was I standing straighter? More confident? Back into the bedroom I stopped and looked at the shape in front of me. My lover, my love. I felt no guilt in the act that just took place and returned to bed beside her.

Olivia's outline was silhouetted against the first hints of morning light coming through the window. Positano faces west so the sun never blinds you in the morning, instead illuminating the rooms as if a dimmer were being pushed up ever so slowly until at full brightness.

I loved her body and how it made me feel, being with her. Never had I felt so complete in sex, equal in giving and receiving. Her smile, her touch, while doing ordinary activities made me warm, inspired me, excited me. She was beside me, with me, as we visited this other world, some portion of it sure to come back with us, even if just the knowing, the shadows of it in our thoughts.

I slowly lowered back onto the bed and rolled to my left behind her. The sheet covered her shape so I slid my hand under and up to her hip, gently resting my palm on her.

Her skin was cool. I looked to the foot of the bed for a blanket and pulled it over us. As I wrapped my arms around her I stopped as my body came in contact with hers.

Cold.

I moved my hands across her, feeling her arms, her chest, her head.

Cold. Motionless.

"Olivia?"

No breathing. No pulse.

Ventisei

CHAPTER TWENTY-SIX

There's a stillness to a dead body. I had never felt it, only seen it at my grandparents' funerals. You can just tell. The lack of air being inhaled and exhaled. Blood not running through veins and arteries.

I was naked kneeling over her, my hands on her shoulders as I screamed her name. Scarlet ran in, Pippo moments later. The light came on and I fell back out of shock. Olivia's face was covered in vomit, her pillow caked and dry with it, yellow and pink.

Pippo pushed me aside, taking my place over her. His fingers pressed against the side of her neck and I saw his shoulders drop, feeling the stillness I had felt. He coupled his hands and began pushing down on the center of her chest. I cursed myself.

"Harder," I said. Her body was barely moving with each compression.

Scarlet was holding my arm, crying, screaming with me.

"I'll call the ambulance." Scarlet turned to leave the room.

"No!" Pippo froze, turned to us. "No."

We looked at him, unable to speak, to fathom why.

He looked down at Olivia again, fingers went to the side of her neck to look for a pulse again. Nothing. He looked deflated, unable to be the master of ceremony, the hero of the moment that he always craved to be.

"No."

"We need to call them." I said.

"We can't."

"Why?" I shoved him off her body and moved to start compressions on her bare chest again. "We have to."

His hands came to mine and stopped them before I could even start, his head moved side to side slowly as he sat back onto the bed.

"She's gone, Avery." He motioned to the dried vomit on the pillow. "It has been hours, probably. She's cold. It's not Olivia anymore."

"We have to try!" I screamed at him. "There's something they can do. There has to be!"

His expression changed from the fear of losing someone to the acceptance of her loss.

"Pippo!" I pleaded as his mood changed.

He stood quickly, taking my shoulders in his hands with force. "Avery, listen to me. This will be difficult to hear, to accept. It would ruin me. My family. And it would ruin you."

Air rushed out of the room. The vacuum left behind was deafening in its silence as I tried to process what he'd said, what was happening, what had happened.

"She's gone, Avery," Pippo said. "She is dead. No phone calls can save her. They can only take away everything else. It would destroy my family, our business."

"What are you talking about? How can you say that right now?"

I had never seen Pippo cry until that moment, whether it was for a friend, a lover lost, or the fear of losing his lifestyle, I didn't know.

He looked down at Olivia, pulled the sheet up over her and got off the bed. Scarlet and I watched as he walked out of the room and to the bar cluttered with empty bottles and dirty glasses. He found a bottle of wine with some left and poured it into a glass and drank it like a shot, then refilled the glass.

"You really think this is the right time for that?" I'd said. "The sun is coming up and my girlfriend is dead and you want to drink?"

Pippo remained silent, his eyes locked on something I couldn't see in the air, behind the walls, past the horizon. He didn't respond to me.

"What the fuck, Pippo!" I screamed at him as I crossed the room. He turned to look at me as my fist struck his face, the first time I ever hit somebody in my life. His body barely moved with the force that brought a stream of bright red blood to his lip with the cracking sounding from my knuckle and the pain that instantly spread through my arm. He didn't react. I tried not to.

I stepped back until I fell onto the sofa where only minutes earlier I had controlled Scarlet. My head turned to the open door to our room. I could just see the end of the bed, the shape of Olivia's foot beneath the sheet. If I hadn't been with Scarlet. If my hand had gone to Olivia when I first woke. Would it have been in time? Could I have seen what was happening? Done something? Saved her?

"What now?" I barely made a sound and wondered for some time if I had before anyone answered.

Scarlet's voice was shaking. "We have to move her."

Pippo and I looked at her.

"Pippo is right. His family name would be ruined. A dead American in their apartment after a wild party. The drugs." She walked to the middle of the room and for the first time I fully realized she was still naked as I was and Pippo as well, my having adjusted to the normalcy of being unclothed. "And what about you, Avery. I don't think parents would want to buy books from you if this got out."

I went from wanting to slap her, knock her to the ground, to knowing she was right faster than I was comfortable with. For the first time I looked at her bare body and saw nothing attractive. I felt nothing sexual, only disgust. I looked at Pippo leaning against the bar, empty wine glass in his hand, his hairy Italian body on full display, the gold Rolex the only thing he wore. His shoulders slumped.

This was his fault. Their fault. The drinking and drugs. The fluidity of bodies and sex. He infected us with his lifestyle, his poison, and it killed Olivia.

I was off the sofa and crossed the dozen feet to him before he even looked up to see me coming. My shoulder struck him in the chest, doubling him back over the bar. We fell to the floor together as I struggled to stay on top of him, throwing punches wherever I could, broken glass cutting us both as I continued to hit him, his face.

He didn't fight back.

After several minutes of striking him I sat on the floor. Scarlet came to my side and knelt down, her hand on my back, her forehead rested on my shoulder.

"Avery," she whispered. I could feel the wetness from her tears on my skin. I wanted to still feel something for her.

"What."

"You should leave," she said.

I pushed her away and stood up, stepping across the room from her. What I thought I knew about her was wrong. Over the weeks together, the nights together, I built her into something she wasn't. She was no better than he was.

"You need to leave. Go home. Get as far away from here as possible. We'll take care of everything." She looked up at Pippo. He was confused at what she was saying, then let it sink in and process. He nodded. Accepted it.

"Leave, Avery," Scarlet said. "And don't come back here."

Ventisette

CHAPTER TWENTY-SEVEN

I sat in the middle of the center section on the connecting flight from Frankfurt, Germany, to New York. A large man on my left, an older woman on my right who spoke no English. I never got out of my seat for the seven hours. I didn't turn on the entertainment screen in the headrest in front of me. Dinner was waved off with a hand and what smile I could muster to keep from seeming rude to the flight attendant who had done nothing wrong.

If you asked me then, somewhere over the Atlantic, how I'd gotten there, I couldn't have answered you. It was scenery in staccato around me, stopping and starting abruptly as I tried to process what happened, what I was going to do next. In the early morning hours after Olivia's death I left the apartment in Positano with my small overnight bag. I'd packed her things up and was carrying it when Scarlet stopped me, gently shaking her head, as she took it from me. I stared at her silently then understood and let it go.

The crowds around me in train stations and airport terminals flowed quickly, unstoppable. Late for a train, I sat on a bench beside the track in Naples for three hours to wait for the next one. Somewhere walking through the airport in Rome I remembered my bag and clothes in an apartment in Florence. I thought about calling Pippo or Scarlet, but I didn't have their phone numbers. Olivia had made the reservations for the trip and paid for them with my credit card through her own email, which I didn't have access to. I didn't even have that email address. Since the night we met we only talked in person, briefly on the phone once perhaps. I don't know. Those are memories pushed further away in their lack of importance compared to the ones made after with her. It was a loose end, something I could do nothing about from this side of the ocean and didn't know yet if it was something that needed attention.

Another connection. Another three hours sitting alone on a crowded flight. I landed in Kansas. Bag claimed. A long taxi ride home. My body wanted to sleep, to have wounds from broken glass tended to, but my brain wouldn't stop for any manner of self-care.

I stood on the sidewalk outside my modest and boring two-story home in the suburbs. The lawn was neatly manicured even after being away for so long, the service I use caring for it. My car was in the garage. It all looked too normal.

The house was musty after sitting empty. I stopped to think how long it had been. A glance at the calendar on the fridge, Olivia's tiny handwriting showing departure times three weeks ago, little loops on her O's making them look almost like tiny 8's.

Three weeks.

That's what it took to change a life. To destroy a life.

Just three weeks.

I scanned the squares to find when we were supposed to have come home, but found no cute scribbles. Only departing on our adventure had mattered to her.

After unpacking I realized there was nothing left of her. Nothing in the house from before. She'd taken everything to Positano with her. She was efficient at packing light and had required only a carry-on sized suitcase for the entire trip. It was the same one she carried with her from Florence to the sea. Now it was gone, too. I didn't know where it went, what they did with it.

Or what they'd done with her.

I didn't want to think about that, but thoughts came to my sleep deprived mind in the middle of the nights, staring at a white ceiling with the hum of the air conditioner filling my ears. My skin formed bumps from the cold circulating around me and I turned the whole system off, opened the windows. The late summer Kansas heat is not like that of Florence. It is moist and heavy and weighs your skin down with humidity.

I knew nothing else about them but their first names. Pippo and Scarlet. Giuseppe was his real name, he'd said the first time we met, and he was from Milan. That's all I could remember. She was from a small town in Holland, I think. I had no way to get ahold of them even if I wanted to.

Olivia had an apartment in Kansas. I'd never been there. Eventually the rent wouldn't be paid and an eviction notice would be stuck to the door. The property manager would go in and her possessions would be packed up and stored or simply thrown in a dumpster. Reveries of her life, perhaps things from her childhood in New York she told me nothing about or photos of her and friends or family. Does she have a sister? A brother? What I didn't know about her burrowed into my being, to the point I couldn't stand to think about them, about her.

I thought about church, going on a Sunday morning or sitting in confession even though I wasn't Catholic. That's what people do when they need help, isn't it? Talk to someone. Share. The need to speak with someone was strong, overbearing. Each night I stared at the row of liquor bottles and wine in the kitchen cabinet, and each time I closed the door without taking any out. I was scared to think what I would do if drunk. Who I might call. Where I might go. What I might say.

Those were all futile thoughts. I had nobody around me. I wasn't going to wander over to a neighbor's house, knock on the door, and say, "Pardon me, may I speak to you about my dead girlfriend?"

I spent one afternoon looking for psychiatrists online, gauging them by their Yelp reviews, before giving up on that thought as well. The story I would tell made no sense and no matter how I thought about it, I came out looking guilty.

One morning I woke up late and found a pair of voice-mails on my phone. The first was from the university, a reminder that faculty meetings for the fall semester were coming up. The second was my agent.

The thought of writing a children's book was foreign, almost disgusting. How could I find that innocence again, that simplicity of the missing library book or stolen dog walking money?

Nothing made sense anymore. To go back to the life I had only six months ago was not an option. Too much had happened. I felt I was changed. Different. Broken.

CHAPTER TWENTY-EIGHT

Sunset in Positano is blocked by land, stealing that one little pleasure of witnessing the sun kiss the sea and melt away. The long light is still brilliant, casting soft shadows across the colorful buildings. I sit at a restaurant by the water and watch the sun disappear over the huge rocky mountain while sipping a mojito. It's not very Italian, but it makes me think of Sara With No H somewhere in Florence, halfway across this long country. For most of the trip down today I regretted not asking her to come with me, to share this place with her. But that would make the purpose of my trip more difficult to carry out.

The past has been a continual flood of memories since arriving. In this small town it is hard not to think of Olivia with every corner, every restaurant, the public swimming area by the dock where we made love in the ocean. Not far behind those are thoughts of Pippo and Scarlet which come with the expected combination of good and bad. When they come to mind I try to concentrate on the times spent with Scarlet, skin on skin, enjoying ourselves, while also remembering that with each day and each replay of the events of our weeks together I am more and more certain they were more than just witnesses to what happened, but instigators, culpable. Guilty.

I assume this is where Pippo and Scarlet were headed when I saw them leave their apartment this morning. They could be anywhere in Europe by now, but this was the only place I knew he might go. If he came by boat again, they should be arriving soon, not far from where I'm sitting. Otherwise, they are somewhere in town or at his apartment. I chose to take the train in order to be ahead of them if they came by sea, missing the chance to see Positano from the water again.

I have no plan, no end game. Countless times I've had conversations in my head, and sometimes out loud at home or in my car, about what I would say to them, to him. I want to know where Olivia is, what was done with her body. The not knowing has burdened me, pulled me down, gnawed at me. The two semesters I taught since last being here were a blur. No faces or names of students remembered. Sleep each night came slowly as I played that one night over and over in my head, of every moment in Italy with Pippo and Scarlet, searching for anything I might have missed. Evidence. Corroboration.

The madness still bubbles beneath my skin and I fight

to keep it at bay. But the anger and frustration and loneliness make anything seem possible, nothing too implausible to be true.

It was six months after returning home before questions that meant something began to form. Ones that could actually be answered. The biggest one was the simplest and shortest.

Why?

I've lived a boring life in a mundane landscape. Commute. Teach. Write. Shop. Repeat. Things that should have been obvious weren't to me while I mourned, screamed, yelled at empty air inside my home. Once I realized what happened, the questions became theories, and my trip back to Italy was to prove them.

The slowest revelation to come was about the missing money from my bank and investment account. I had assumed a random act at first, a skilled criminal either in Italy or even in Kansas that had gained access to my information. Eventually, the coincidence of it gave way to suspicion, then a feeling deep inside of the truth.

Pippo stole my money and killed Olivia as a distraction, a way to get rid of me. It was the perfect crime. I was too slow in realizing it was him that had drained my accounts, and even when I considered the possibility, I didn't think he was smart enough. I wondered why he hadn't killed me, leaving no one behind to suspect him, to call the police on him.

He got about $232,000. Was that worth it to him? It was all my liquid savings and the one investment account

I kept at my primary credit union. Far more was locked in other banks.

A woman walks past and a scent hits my nose. The same perfume Sara wears. I turn quickly in my chair only to find it isn't her. I feel calm with Sara, more so than I have been in months. My desire to get answers is still there but my patience is stronger.

Sara centers me. Being away from her, or being so close to where Olivia died, I'm losing control. I can feel the anger growing that had been muted, dulled in the days and nights with Sara.

The sun is gone along with the soft glow of orange light. With the anonymity of darkness, I walk through town. The restaurants are busy. Lights, music, and voices spill out onto the street as I pass. At one curve in the road I pause as I imagine the song Scarlet had heard in her head that night when I told her I wanted to kiss her on this very spot.

Pippo and Scarlet are the flame that moths fly to, want to be near, crave, even if they know they will get burned.

In junior high I made friends with a new kid in school for a short time. It was rare for me to click with someone and I grabbed on. After school one day I went to his house to watch television with him. He had a dog, a small bulldog of some kind. It was ugly and drooled a lot. He would pick the dog up and throw it halfway across the room, landing with a thud, knocking over a small table at one point, all while reruns of Magnum P.I. blared in the background. But the dog would jump up and run back to him, eager to be played with, even though it hurt. I pulled away after that, seeing how he treated something he cared about. I see Pippo as similar to him. He treats people in his orbit however he wants, making them part of his world superficially, momentarily, enough to tempt them with that life to the point they will do things they never had.

Farther away from the nightlife, the town is quiet as locals settle in for the evening. I see more than I had before when I was only watching the two women in my life at the time. Darkened doors to homes built into the land spot the walls. Through a window I see a family eating in front of a small television. They don't have big comfortable sofas. They sit on wooden chairs, the children on the floor. And they look happy.

It is so easy to visit a place we consider perfect, paradise, without thinking about those who live there and raise families. Locals who work in the shops for other people, sweeping floors and making coffee, delivering packages and fixing plumbing. We don't want to think about the normal side of paradise, just the beaches and drinks and great meals and sex. But that's what we expect from vacation, an escape from what we live day after day at home, to be the ones waited on and catered to, cared for and thanked.

Pippo straddles that line, a foot firmly on either side of being a tourist and a local. But he acts the role of the perpetual vacationer with no base in the real world. He doesn't work and only takes from others.

I stop walking and move to a shadow on my right, a dark spot between two streetlights, and look up at the apartment.

Lights are on. It is a long time, but finally there is motion, a shape passes the near window, obscured by the thin curtain. I'm glued, unable to move my feet or divert my eyes. Anyone walking by would have thought me a statue. I know that I won't leave, that I will be here until I see him, see them. The hotel room I rented would house only my suitcase.

Just over a year ago I walked this same street, slept in that apartment. And just over a year ago I found my girlfriend dead beside me in the guest suite. It is something that has not left me, and I feel never will, no matter what happiness I may find. Olivia woke me to emotions I never thought I could feel, to pleasures I had never known and some I never expected to know. She broke me out of hibernation, the fog of life that kept me hidden, safe. Before her I went day to day, teaching and writing, with nothing but drives to the grocery store and to see my parents in between. I had thought I was happy but was just content. I was settled.

Olivia gave me happiness and travel and laughter and love. She broke me out of the routine and mundane and into a real existence, one where I felt I mattered for those months together, before.

The door to the building slams closed before I know what's happening. I flatten my body to the building, hidden in a corner between two homes. I hear footsteps but don't lean out to look, instead waiting. I hold my breath for fear the exhalation could be heard in the still night.

Then he passes, unaware of my presence, no idea I am

feet away. For a moment I don't know why I'm hiding. I came to talk to him, to fight with him, to fill in the blanks that have been bothering me for a year. Instead I am hiding in a shadow.

He is looking down at his phone as he walks away, tapping crazily at the keyboard with one hand, a small duffle bag hangs low in the other. For the first time I realize I rarely saw him with a phone. His attention had always been on Olivia and me. I could walk right past him and he wouldn't notice. Once he is gone around the curve, I fall in behind him.

The roads wind up and down the hill with very few hard corners. It is easy to stay near him and have the cover of the buildings. When I lose sight for more than a few seconds, I take several quicker steps and get another glimpse.

A few other people are out. Some strolling as lovers, others are groups of friends traveling together, drinking together. Nobody catches Pippo's eye and I avoid being noticed by them.

It's nearly midnight as we approach the water. The open square by the dock provides less cover and I follow the walls to my right as Pippo continues down the middle of the road. He taps at his keyboard again, looking up at the water and back at his phone. Once to the edge of the dock he sets the duffle bag down and puts the phone in his pocket.

I maneuver to the corner of the building under an awning where all light is blocked. After a glance around to see if anyone else is near, I kneel down beside a table from the closed café.

Pippo just stands, staring at the water, hands in his pockets. He is too far away, maybe it is the breeze off the ocean carrying it, but I swear I can smell his stink that turned my stomach the first day we met at the *Accadamie*. A bare bulb hangs from a wire above him, casting harsh shadows of his shape on the concrete, three versions of him spread out on the ground, the fourth lost in the darkness of the water. He pulls his left hand out of his pocket and raises his arm. The light flashes off the face of the Rolex as he checks the time.

I think of the story he and Scarlet told us that first evening of how they met in Amsterdam. It had always seemed scripted, rehearsed. When she spoke out of turn, he glared at her. He'd been mugged in a dark alley, his wallet and his phone stolen. But he still has the Rolex he received when he graduated university.

That god damned Rolex.

My thoughts are interrupted with the drone of an engine. A light bobs in the water until a boat pulls up to the dock. Pippo catches a rope thrown to him and wraps it around the metal cleat mounted in the cement. A man jumps from the boat onto dry land in dark shorts and a matching jacket. When he turns toward the light, it shines off his whisky blond hair and I see it is Vincent, the skipper.

I want to hear them but there is nowhere else to hide between me and them. From Pippo's body I can tell he isn't happy. A few times his voice rises, but I can tell they are speaking in Italian and are still too far away. Vincent looks defensive, then lowers his head, and grabs a flat black bag from the boat and gives it to Pippo. Pippo hands him the duffle bag and slaps him on the shoulder, then points out into the blackness of the sea.

The duffle is tossed onto the boat we'd taken to Capri, and Vincent jumps on as Pippo releases the rope and tosses it to the skipper. Once the boat has motored out into the water, Pippo turns and walks within ten feet of me and back up into town.

CHAPTER TWENTY-NINE

The black Mercedes S350 sedan takes the curves from Positano to Sorrento effortlessly as I ride in the back seat. I look through the side windows to the sea on my left without taking it in, my thoughts instead on Pippo. I had followed him home then retreated to my hotel, certain all activity for the night was over. Unable to sleep, I was back outside before the sun rose only to see Pippo and Scarlet coming down the street toward me, bags in hand. I moved quickly onto a side street and waited until they passed, then watched them board the first ferry to Sorrento, then likely the train to Naples, Rome, then Florence once again. I already had the number for a car service in case I needed to leave quickly, and called it.

It is another calculated decision on where they are going. They traveled light to Positano, only small handbags with them, so returning to their home in Florence seems likely. An overnight trip to the sea is odd, but framed with whatever business he had with Vincent can explain it.

Leaving Positano feels wrong. It is where I thought I would end the trip, where answers would be found, accusations made. Perhaps I just wanted more time there to think of Olivia in the last place I'd seen her alive.

The Mercedes drops me at the Napoli Centrale terminal and I am grateful to skip the *Circumvesuviana* train to get here. I buy a ticket and watch closely for Pippo and Scarlet in case they are traveling by train and have made it here at the same time, though I feel I should be well ahead of them. I choose the lower priced fare for an economy cabin, knowing he would pay for the nicer business class with bigger seats and no children.

I lean back in my seat and watch out the window as Naples is left behind along with views of Mount Vesuvius. The urban landscape of low concrete buildings fades into the rolling hills. It makes me want to love Italy again, to travel her and take in her sights and flavors. But I feel that won't be happening after this trip. I don't see how I could ever be here again and enjoy myself. There are other parts of the world to explore once I am ready.

People walk past me down the aisle and I turn to see them as they go through the door into the next car as I watch for Pippo. A small television hangs from the ceiling playing ads, weather, and news clips with no volume as subtitles in Italian stream at the bottom of the screen. A story about upcoming elections ends and goes into one showing a small boat on fire. As the subtitles flash by, I think I see the name Vincent, but it is gone before I can try to decipher the foreign language.

With my phone, I search local news sources and find one reporting the story. My fingers mistype, eager to tap out the words. There are more photos of the boat, badly burned and drifting at sea as a rescue ship is nearby. I tap to translate the story to English.

"The small craft was spotted engulfed in flames off the coast south of Amalfi. The registration of the boat is to Vincent Costa, but attempts to contact him have failed."

I feel my body heat rise and sweat form on my face. I run through what I saw last night. Pippo at the dock with Vincent. The duffle bag, not anything I'd seen him carry before. He hadn't brought it with him from Florence. A heated discussion.

His guilt was cementing in my mind with no judge or jury, only my thoughts and instincts condemning him. First Olivia, now Vincent, likely the only other person who knew where her body ended up.

My distrust and fear of Pippo is heightened. I know I should reevaluate my vague plans to confront him, beg him for answers. Accuse him. But I'm only more intent on doing so. I know there will be a place and a time that I can catch him off guard, unprepared for me and for the interrogation. I imagine everything from simple to crazy, running the gamut from sitting at his table at a restaurant and asking him point blank to hiring some locals from a seedy bar to help capture him, tie him up in a dirty backroom and yell questions at him, threatening bodily harm. Or do I wait until he's several bottles of wine into a night of reveling, perhaps even floating from another dose of Ecstasy that allows his mouth to act freely of his brain.

Follow through is my greatest fault. It isn't one you can say out loud in an interview when they ask you the clichéd question, as if anyone will actually say it.

I walk past their apartment in Florence after sunset, obscured in the shadows across the street. Lights are on. No motion. I wait at the busy café where I can see the road they always walk down. Slowly sipping wine, I watch the street as I think about what I'm going to do. I can only follow them so long.

That night in Positano is still vivid in my memories. Her cold skin against my hands. The silence of her body. When I stood above her, fingers clasped and pushing down on her chest, I thought I'd seen something, a spark, some life. I think about it often and try to place what it was. A movement of her mouth? Did her eyelids flicker momentarily? Anything I may have seen was an illusion or an involuntary act of her body, muscles being forced into motion by the artificial pumping of blood from pressing down on her. It had given me hope in that moment even though I had felt her body and seen the vomit she had likely choked on in her sleep.

A year later I hope that it wasn't real, that she had been gone before I woke and found her. I couldn't live with knowing there had been a chance, that one more compression might have sent the spark that her heart and brain needed to kick on again. That would be too much to handle.

I've finished two glasses of wine when I see them. They walk down the other side of the small street, him a half step ahead of her. There's no hand holding or affection between them, which makes me look again to confirm it is them.

With money left on the table, I set out to follow them. I can see the reflection of her glittery blouse two blocks down and maintain some distance. My heart pounds as I give measured chase, not wanting to get too close. I try to go over my options, my endgame, but nothing comes. I'm just walking, following. I feel my anger coming out, the urge to run, to catch them, to hurt him. We'd fought that night Olivia died but he hadn't retaliated, letting my strikes land without defense. It won't be like that again if we come face to face. He's bigger and stronger than I am. Unlike me, he has no fear.

A right turn then a left. A fine layer of sweat coats my face and chest as I keep my pace up to match theirs on the hot night. They are out of sight for a few minutes after making a turn. As I come around the same corner I stop short and push myself to the wall.

They aren't there. I try to control my breathing to hear around me, take everything in to see what I missed, scanning through the scattered reflections and shadows of glowing yellow streetlights. I turn to look behind me. Did they double back, knowing someone was following? No movement in the darkness. Other people walk by, paying me no attention.

For a moment I hear music, then it goes away. Four people appear on the sidewalk a block down. Their voices travel, reflecting off the stone walls, and I hear muffled drunken conversations.

I set off again, keeping my senses heightened to watch for them, listen for them. Smell them. The loud music comes again as I near the group on the sidewalk. More people stumble out.

I don't know the restaurant. Looking around, the street isn't familiar, so we'd never ventured to this part of town before. The windows are frosted so I wait until the door opens again to get an idea of how large it is before I enter, not wanting to step in and have eyes on me. A couple comes down the sidewalk. The man opens the door and lets the young woman pass and I strain my neck to see over them.

From the street, the room looks long. Lights hang from the ceiling giving perspective on the distance. As the door swings shut, I grab it and enter behind the man and woman as cover.

There is no fear of being noticed. It is crowded and loud and smells of sweat and spilled liquor. For a space in Florence, it is large. Though there are people eating dinner, it is more of a club than a restaurant. People stand everywhere, talking, drinking. The bar is a rectangle in the middle, running most of the length with multiple bartenders pouring drinks. I move down the right side of the bar, watching the crowds drinking and talking as I go, pulling the brim lower on my hat to conceal myself. I know the glittery gold blouse Scarlet is wearing and hope it will stand out enough for me to see them before they see me.

It takes fifteen minutes to work my way around once, slowed by gangs of partiers and taking my time to not appear as if I'm searching for someone. As I get around to the other side with no sight of them, I take the one empty stool I see at the bar and order a drink. Another mojito to think of Sara. An eye roll from the man who takes my order.

Through the movement of the bartenders I watch the other side of the room for flashes of gold, or to hear the deep voice of Pippo rise above everyone. It is inevitable. He will demand the room bow to him, but still nothing.

I feel consumed by the motion and noise around me, jetsam pulled from the safety of shore into the tide and thrown around. When I was at Olivia's side I could handle these places. I'd been able to focus on her, filtering out the sound except for her voice, orbiting in her gravitational pull. As much as I've grown, changed, the chaos of noise and smells still brings my anxiety to the surface, slows my reaction.

The drink is placed in front of me and I put my attention on it, the beads of sweat rolling down the outside of the tall glass, a single piece of mint crushed and floating among the few ice cubes. Expectations are low. A sip. No taste of rum. No taste at all, for that matter. The bartender is gone to the other end, avoiding eye contact, likely not wanting to spend the time making another mixed drink while focusing on the beautiful women who smile while ordering Prosecco and white wine.

I feel out of place among the party people; the young and gorgeous, the rich and those who stay in their circle to feed off of them, off their energy and their money. I want it to be over. I need to be done chasing. Several times on the trip I've wondered for the briefest moments what getting answers would do for me. What blaming him for Olivia's death could possibly do. Would it make the pain go away? It wouldn't bring her back. It feels wrong to forget about her, to leave her memory and her body to the murky depths of the sea or wherever she ended up and move on. The love I had for her won't let me do that no matter how much I doubt myself or my ability to follow through. I settle in everything I do. No great masterpieces written, only children's books. I don't care about the money he stole. Insurance recouped most of it and my books continue to create income.

In the dark hours of the night standing outside Pippo's apartment in Positano, I wondered if meeting Sara had changed things for me more than I want to accept. Did I just need a smiling face and soft lips to kiss, a beautiful body to make love to? I can't think that I'm that shallow, that needy, that one could replace another so easily. Is that what six months is worth in mourning? A year. All-in-all only a fraction of my 36 years alive.

"*Tre bicchieri di Prosecco, por favore.*"

The voice comes over my right shoulder, the Italian language wrapped in a non-native accent. My nerve endings light up, and my body turns cold as I fight to not move, not turn, not look. I can smell her, the perfume she always wears.

Scarlet.

For an instant I was back in that apartment in Positano, naked with her, controlling her, feeling her gorgeous black skin against me, her body wrapped around me. The smell of her perfume had been strong that night, that morning, it blurred in my mental timeline of events, for only minutes later I discovered Olivia.

The bartender pulls a cork on a new bottle in an endless process of showing off to pour three glasses of the bubbly gold liquid to a beautiful woman. I am static, immobile. I realize I have my drink raised halfway to my mouth and finally take a sip. I lower it, spinning the square napkin before setting the glass down just as I realize I always do that, it's a tell I never noticed about myself until sitting here right now, and force myself to stop in the chance she notices, recognizes the mannerism, or just takes a second look at me.

I inhale and take in her perfume. It had intoxicated me once as I craved her touch, tasted her skin. With her it had been just physical. A lust, an impure desire, setting it apart from my love for Olivia and allowing me to be with them both, separately and together. My emotions for each were strong but polar opposite. One I wanted to live with, wake up with, make love to, and spend the rest of my years with. The other I wanted to experience, an exotic beauty not meant to be tamed or ever settle down.

Glasses are placed on the bar, overfilled as they do for the attractive people who order and smile and flip their hair. A glimpse to my side without turning my head. Still I resist the urge to fully look at her. From this close she would surely recognize me. We had been much closer before. She's beside me. Our skin touches momentarily in the incidental action of reaching for drinks, leaving money on the bar, an offhanded *pardon me* delivered with that hint of a dialect from a small town in Holland.

The scent of her perfume fades and she's gone. I can't think of Scarlet without thinking of Olivia. One does not exist without the other in my memory, even though I'd known Olivia longer.

I am now locked in my seat, not knowing where she is, where they are. Behind me. Beside me. I could turn and be facing them or they might be lost in the crowd. It was a chance I wasn't willing to take, not yet.

He has me nervous now. Scared of him. I found him annoying at first but harmless. In the news of Vincent's death and my suspicions that grew daily that he had stolen my money, and the mere suggestion that he killed Olivia, my anxiety grows. I swallow the last of the watered-down drink and motion to the bartender for another.

CHAPTER THIRTY-ONE

Olivia would hold me from behind in bed, the reverse spoon, she called it. It was satisfying and warm. I felt you can be held by someone you care about but only hold someone you love. Her arm would come over my side, hand flat on my chest, pulling me toward her so tightly I believed I could feel her heartbeat.

I could live in those moments. She found little things, gentle touches, simple words, that kept me surprised by her. In love with her. In awe of her. These are the things I miss the most. The little things.

After our first night together, we were not apart again unless I was in class or she was at work. She would come home with wine and I would cook. We would eat sitting on the living room floor or on the back deck under the rust orange umbrella. On the weekends she was happiest staying home or going for walks in the parks and on trails near my house.

I had a book signing event in Tulsa and she went with

me. She watched from the back row at a small bookstore while I spoke to the loud children and their parents who brought them to see me. I answered the same questions that were always asked. There were the typical kid questions that were generally way too specific about a small part of a single book. *Did Simon the cat get to eat the mouse?* Or the generic ones obviously put into their mouths by parents. *What inspired you to write books?*

I sat with Olivia on the patio of a restaurant later that night, drinking wine and talking softly. She never sounded uninterested in anything we spoke about.

"You handle the children well," she said.

"I've gotten used to them. Wasn't always easy. To be honest, I'm not much of a kid person."

She laughs through a sip of wine. "And you write children's books?"

"Go figure, right?"

"Is this what you wanted?"

"What do you mean?"

"To be a successful author of more than twenty children's mystery novels." She said it like she was reading my bio off the back cover.

It's something I'd thought about a lot but nobody had ever asked me. "No. I don't mind it, but I originally wanted to write novels, of course."

"Why don't you?"

"It's hard once you're established in one genre, especially children's books, to write something different."

"Then use your own name."

"I've considered that. I guess I just haven't found the right story to tell yet."

She was turned in her seat, a leg pulled up under her so she was leaning to her side, looking at me.

"You're scared to."

She always saw right through me.

"Yeah. I am. Writing for kids isn't easy, but they are certainly less discerning than their parents, or book critics."

"I want you to try."

"Why?"

"Because I know that you want to try."

"It's not that simple."

"It can be."

CHAPTER THIRTY-TWO

I hear him.

It comes for a moment, a beacon moving, disappearing into fog and thunder, until it is there again and I strain to make it constant, tilting my head, closing my eyes, targeting him, tuning it in.

The room is larger and louder than he usually commands, making it more difficult to be the center, to draw the attention he craves. Sometimes it takes a while, depending on the group, but he always does. He isn't too close, I can tell, so I pick up my drink and turn slowly on the rotating barstool, surveying the crowd. I sip. An attempt at blending in.

The monotonous drone of electronic rhythms occupies the air of the restaurant as bodies move in time, whether intentional or not. It is the pulse of the room, designed to keep people up, excited, thirsty. There are no melodies I can decipher, just noise.

In my mind I stand out for my stillness, obvious

in my inability to blend in, to enjoy life along with everyone else. A death grip on my drink glass. I focus on the noises below the wavelengths of the electronica, the voices and laughter behind me, working to pinpoint and isolate the sounds.

My hat is tipped down on my brow, obscuring my face, my beard and drink covering the bottom half. It's the disguise I unknowingly created over the months before returning. I feel incognito from a distance but my charade, my new and marginally improved persona, will not hold up face-to-face in close quarters. I somehow survived the run in with him outside the restaurant but won't be that lucky again. I need to catch him off guard, not get noticed from across a crowded room, giving him the opportunity to strike first, or to run.

It's like the first night back with Sara all over, hearing him, then watching the crowd for a glimpse. It doesn't take long before I see him above the rest, his height a disadvantage. The green shirt again. The glass of Prosecco in his hand. He raises his elbows and does a satirical dance move, something likely spawned by a comment from Scarlet. The mating dance of the nearly extinct Italian boor.

And there she is, by his side, smiling at him, directing him, encouraging him. Her skin glows in the lights, or maybe just appears to. Through everything there is still an attraction, an exotic nature to her that pulls me, something erotic and sensual. I want to hate her as much as I hate him. But I can't. I tell myself she was an unwilling partner to whatever happened, another of Pippo's pawns pulled into his game. Even so, she knows whatever he knows and is just as guilty.

Maybe she is the answer. Do I get her alone, talk to her, get her to turn on her lover? Watching her watch him, though, I know that is unlikely. He may be the charisma and the money, but she pulls the strings. I see it more clearly, that he was created from her attraction to him, his desire to entertain her and amuse her. They are a single entity now, neither possess power without the other.

A momentary wave of dizziness. I look down at my drink and wonder if it was stronger than I'd first thought as I find myself standing at the edge of the crowd surrounding Pippo. He is so close that if he turned, it would be hard not to recognize me. If I spoke his name, he would hear me.

I feel out of control of my actions, pulled by a force I can't see. My subconscious thoughts are taking over, doing what I have wanted to do for so long. Another step closer. Another drink. That's the only thing I can control right now and I take advantage, swallowing as much of the liquor that I can as each step brings me closer to answers. To confrontation. To…I don't know what. The time is upon me and I still don't know what I'm going to say, hours of rehearsing in bathroom mirrors and sitting at red lights, points made and accusations leveled in imaginary conversations. In my thoughts I always won, defeating him mentally until he breaks, tells me everything, though I never hear the confession in my rehearsals. That is all that is left, to hear him speak, to say it, say something. To show some remorse, to cave in and cry. I don't know. I don't care. I just need a reaction, something to cement my feelings for him and to frame my emotions for Olivia in better light, out from under the shadow of the accusation of murder.

Scarlet is dancing around him, her hands running over his body while he spins the other direction, his arms in the air. She's mocking his dance while urging him on. Her movement pulls me in and I watch her arms, her hips. I so want to hate her. To despise her as much as I do him, but I can't.

Another pair of hands from the group orbiting them joins hers in their made-up May Day celebration, blonde and black hair alternating in rotations around his body, faster and faster until as if rehearsed, the two women stop.

I'm five feet from them.

Scarlet laughs and I hear her so clearly. The sound strokes memories I hadn't summoned in some time. Enjoyment, fun, sex. Late nights in Positano, in Florence. At bars and on the floor of their apartment. She wraps her arms around the other woman and as they spin I look at the blonde hair and the bare shoulders coming out from the thin strapped red dress as the woman turns and...

Olivia.

CHAPTER THIRTY-THREE

My fingers lose their grip on the glass in my hand. It shatters on the floor. The sound pierces the music and voices and pulls attention from Pippo. A dozen people look at the floor as broken glass and ice gets kicked underfoot by the constant motion of bodies. Women dancing barefoot are moving to avoid the shards but can't avoid stepping on them, screams of pain. I am lost in the chaos and step back, a curtain of people passing in front of me.

I can't stop staring, wondering if it is really her. The hair is wrong but everything else is Olivia. Still so beautiful.

Through the growing crowd between us her gaze meets mine and a confused look crosses her face. There is a knowing in her look. A recognition. A fear, perhaps. Her eyes don't leave mine while Pippo and Scarlet move around her with the others, in between us, revolving around her, kicking broken glass away and carrying shoeless girls out of the way as she stands still. She won't stop looking at me, or can't, as I can't either.

A year of knowing she is dead. Of missing her and wanting answers. Of blaming Pippo. Of blaming myself. And here she is in front of me, very much alive. I'm paralyzed, unable to move or speak, not knowing what I would say if I could. The few feet between us is an uncrossable void, an impossible reach into the dark to pull someone back from the dead. Never had I imagined what I would say to her if ever she stood before me again. It wasn't a possibility. There was no logic in putting those words or thoughts together. She wasn't an ex-girlfriend I pined after, dreaming of getting back with. I didn't pass her on the street, bump into her at the grocery store with an awkward hello. She was dead. I'd felt her cold body against mine. I want to rush to her, grab her in my arms, tell her I love her. Kiss her. Feel her warm skin once more to wash away the endless memory of her coldness.

As quickly as being with her again takes over my thoughts, my body regains control and I step backwards. She's alive. I held her dead body. I cried for her, screamed for her, as Pippo and Scarlet told me to leave that night, and I had. I left her.

She was dead. I know she was. But there was that glimmer, that spark I had seen when my hands pushed on her chest. Was it real? Pippo had knelt over her on the bed, taken control, and I watched him try to save her while I stood helpless, his compressions too gentle, too shallow, I thought at the time, but the words not coming out of me.

Then he had stopped, covered her with a dramatic lift of the sheet, over her body, her head. She was dead. The air billowed beneath the sheet and finally settled, forming to her shape. We left the room and I never walked back in. I never checked her again. I never said goodbye.

All of the memories speed by as I continue to look at her and her at me. My body turns as cold as hers was that early morning, a chill down my spine as thoughts form and merge. Pippo grabs her arm, spinning her back to the party with the commotion shoved to the side. The women with glass shards in their feet removed, forgotten about. As Olivia glances back over her shoulder at me one more time the thoughts collide and become real. They become what must be the truth, the only truth that makes sense with her being in front of me now, being with him. I am angered and embarrassed at my own ignorance, standing there in front of its proof. The loud music has muted the voices in front of me now, even Pippo's absent from the spectrum. *Did he see me?*

I turn and rush through the crowd. The exit seems miles away but I finally reach it and push. I don't look back again, afraid of the darkness I now know is behind me. The evil.

It had all been a lie, from the moment I saw her in the bookstore to every time we made love or spent long evenings holding each other in the quiet of my home. I had handed her my credit cards, access to my bank accounts to plan the trip. I had paid for my own fate, the pain I felt for so long, the guilt of being party to her death. We didn't run into Pippo and Scarlet on accident at the museum. I played my part in their script, reading along word for word, never straying, feeding right into them.

My eyes are wet, the emotions striking me hard from the realizations of all the lies, the grift. It was in that moment I lost her for the second time, and lost all of the moments we had shared, the memories that had pulled me through the year of not having her with me anymore. They were all lies.

Through the door I stagger, half running, half falling. My arms flail to grab hold of something, anything, to avoid hitting the ground, and my hand strikes skin. A grunt of pain, of surprise, as the other body is now moving with me, spinning.

I grip an arm to slow my motion, to try to control us both, then get my legs beneath me again while my head continues to spin.

My head down, eyes still blurred. "I'm sorry." I turn to run and three steps on my way when I hear the voice.

"Avery?"

It doesn't register at first as I move on, hurrying to get away from the one person I'd wanted to see again for over a year but knew I could not. It was impossible. My body shivers as I think of her cold skin on mine, the dried vomit. The deception.

"Avery!"

I stop but don't turn. Footsteps from behind. A hand comes to my arm. I'm not prepared for this. How could anyone.

"Are you okay?"

The melody of the words relaxes me, comforts me, as I take my first breath since seeing Olivia. The voice behind me is sweetness and caring.

I turn and look at Sara.

"Take me home," I say. "Please. Get me out of here."

With no hesitation she goes into motion and I move along beside her with no effort as if she is carrying me, but I know she is not. Her will and her affection is strong, encompassing. At the next corner we turn and she waves her arm to a passing taxi.

An address is given and I realize it is mine as the car speeds off. I turn and look out the rear window. Nobody is on the curb. Nobody is chasing.

"What's going on?" She says.

My vision is cloudy as my heart thumps hard inside my chest. Fingers numb. I can't breathe.

"I don't feel— "

The room glows with the morning sun reflecting in from the terracotta roofs. I lie still, not remembering how I got here, to my own apartment. Images come to me in dull flashes, memories working themselves through my grogginess.

Olivia.

She's alive. The brief flash of happiness is replaced by the rest of it, the deceit, the lies, and I will myself not to cry.

I startle at a sound from the other room, then Sara comes in with a glass of water. She is beautiful in the avocado dress I last saw her in, when I intended never to see her again.

"You're here," I say.

"I am."

"How did you get me upstairs?"

"Let's just say I tipped the taxi driver really well."

"The taxi." I look to the brightness of the window to try to remember.

Sara leans me forward with the abrupt gentleness of a nurse and pushes a pillow up against the headboard and leans me against it. Another pillow is placed beside me, trying to brace me from falling over. Every muscle feels as if it has been pushed to failure. My equilibrium is gone. I'm exhausted and sore. It's worse than the mornings after the pills Pippo would get for us.

"That's above and beyond. I don't know what happened to me."

"That was what you call a panic attack."

"Really? How do you know?"

"My sister is a doctor. I called her."

"In Ireland?"

"London, actually."

"I don't know what to say."

"I do." She sits on the edge of the bed and turns to me. "What?"

"Everything. You've been acting all cloak and dagger since I first met you. I'm a good judge of character so I went along with it because you're cute and you make me smile. But it's time to come clean."

"What do you mean?"

"What are you doing in Italy?" she says. "And who is that man? I saw him there last night, the same one from the café last week and outside that restaurant a couple nights later."

I attempt to look like I don't know what she's talking about and fail.

"Three times we've seen them and three times you acted oddly, or worse."

She has me cornered and at this point I wonder if it really matters.

"Buy me breakfast and I'll tell you everything."

CHAPTER THIRTY-FOUR

I've spent my life looking for a rhythm. A pace. As a child, it made sense to me that the world had a heartbeat, just like humans and animals. We built civilizations, our modern world, around the ticking of a clock. An artificial heartbeat. It never felt natural. I would listen to music, tapping along, song to song, trying to find what felt right. Different songs would give me different feelings, different emotions, and I felt it was the rhythm as much as, if not more than, the melody and lyrics.

When I was about ten years old I wanted to conduct orchestras. I would put my parent's old albums on the record player and stand in the living room, my arms flailing about, having no idea how to actually conduct an orchestra. For some time I thought the musicians followed the baton and got their music from it. The higher the baton, the higher the notes, the speed dictated by the velocity of the flicks of the wrist, controlling the rhythm.

After joining band in junior high and choosing the trumpet as my instrument, I quickly learned I had no talent for music. This was a blow to me. I tried as hard as I could. Locked in my room, I worked through the sheet music, attempting to make something that sounded melodic. But I couldn't. I quit after one year and my parents sold the trumpet back for far less than they'd paid for it. I never asked to join anything else after that.

Those albums collected dust again as they had for years before I rediscovered them. I couldn't listen to them anymore. They reminded me of letting my parents down, and letting myself down.

I was walking through the school library sometime after that, running my fingers across the spines of the books. Some were wrapped in clear plastic protecting the dust jackets. An off-white cover with brown calligraphy lettering caught my eye. The design was simple. A line drawing of a man and a dog and a camper.

I opened the book and began reading. I found something I hadn't expected, that I hadn't experienced in the books assigned in school. A rhythm.

The next three days were spent reading that book whenever I had the chance until it was done. Back at the library I found the same author and checked out two more books. *Cannery Row* and *Sweet Thursday*. They had a different rhythm than the first, *Travels with Charley*. It set the tone for the words. And it would change, speeding up or slowing down to guide the reader through emotions.

I returned the books and thought about them for a week before opening to an empty page of a notebook and writing my own first story. It wasn't very good, but it had a rhythm. It had what I'd been searching for.

That began me on the path to becoming a writer. I had bigger plans, to be a novelist and write big sweeping stories that pulled readers in and made them look for the next one, just as I had with Steinbeck. My parents' desire for me to go into a professional field in college was left behind, choosing a liberal arts school and four years of undergrad then a Masters of Fine Arts for creative writing.

After a few boxes full of rejection letters from agents and publishers, I went back to my old notebooks. I saw a simplicity in them that I had lost. The stories were basic, a three-piece band compared to the symphonies I was trying to compose with the novels as an adult.

My life found its own beat. It was slow and steady, never getting too complicated or hectic. I teach. I write. It's comfortable. Easy.

Until I met Olivia. In the first moments of talking to her I felt a disruption. A new tempo. It was exciting and soothing at the same time.

CHAPTER THIRTY-FIVE

I open a third bottle of wine and pour a full glass. Some of the red liquid sloshes over the edge and drips down onto the dark brown dresser in my apartment. I make no attempt to wipe it up. The streetlights cast a glow across the room, the only illumination I'll allow. My head isn't right from the first two bottles and I hope the third does me in for the night. I need to sleep and push everything away.

I sat at a table across from Sara with cappuccino and croissants this morning while I told her the entire story, from the first time I saw Olivia at the book signing in Kansas, up to last night. No detail was left out. Broad strokes were questioned and broken down into individual moments to give the full picture until I was done, emotionally and physically spent from reliving more than a year over the course of my coffee growing cold.

"And you're sure that was her in the restaurant last night?" she said.

"Positive."

"She's alive."

"Seems that way."

"You know what that means?"

"I do."

We talked a bit more. She listened. Then she was gone. It wasn't in anger or hatred. Disappointment, perhaps, that I hadn't been honest. I don't think she blames me for not telling her the truth when we first met. That is understandable. I think she left for fear of being caught in the middle. For being mistaken as part of everything that has happened. I don't blame her. Olivia would tell Pippo she saw me. He might come after me, to hurt me, or worse. It's a lot for Sara to take in, to process. We met a week ago but both feel far more connected than the calendar alludes to. At least I am.

This is how it's supposed to be, anyway. My plan didn't involve anyone else. I let myself get distracted by her and fumbled through the trip. There are even more things I don't know now about Pippo and Scarlet, and now Olivia.

Through the telling Sara had asked questions and pointed things out I hadn't thought of. The only time I recall Pippo doing anything that seemed to relate to money was the morning we left for Capri. He had been writing in that leather book then put it back in his suitcase, hidden beneath his clothing.

There are no answers I need anymore. Sure, I would like to hear their reason, but it is likely a simple one.

For money. For fun. Because they can. After Sara walked away this morning, I called the airline and booked my return flight home on the next available flight out of Rome tomorrow afternoon.

I want to be done with this place. With Florence. With Italy. It no longer holds a spell over me as it had standing in the rain or staring up at stars with Olivia. But mostly I want to be done with Pippo. Not long ago I was eager to stand face to face with him, to confront him with questions. Just the thought of it brought his sharp musk to mind, too vivid from my memories of all the time spent close to him, too close.

In junior high there was a coach who always had a stink to him. Though it was likely his armpits, it seemed to emanate from his clothes, from his whole body. He walked around smiling, happy to be alive and more than happy to make us run laps, wrestle, and climb ropes to touch the gym ceiling. I don't know if he ever knew what the kids said about him, the names we called him. If so, he never let on.

"If they did this to you, they've done it before," Sara had said after my story. "And they'll do it again."

That thought has had me reeling all day since she left and through the wine, inspiring the drinking. I now just want to get on an airplane and go live my boring life again. I've never imagined myself a hero or someone to seek revenge, but also never saw myself as a victim.

And they'll do it again.

The words stick in my brain, rolling over and over.

Another glass, red stains on my shirt. I hide in my apartment, suitcase packed and ready for the morning taxi to the airport. They're out there somewhere. They're spending my money, and likely the money of others they cheated as they had me. Their ruse plays over and over in my mind as I look for signs I surely missed, that others have surely missed.

And they'll do it again.

Olivia's body on the bed in Positano, the crusty vomit on her mouth.

How many times has Olivia died?

And they'll do it again.

CHAPTER THIRTY-SIX

The night continues to slip past me while I go between staring at the ceiling and being passed out from the wine. Even with the thin curtains pulled, Florence continues its momentum outside my window as it has since the Romans walked the streets. Tourists stare in awe at the architecture while locals react with the same nonchalance as when you walk past a Starbuck's at home. I want to be secluded, away from the world, from Florence, from Pippo, and from Olivia.

Oh, Olivia. I should be excited you are alive. Eager to hold you and kiss you. Instead I'm afraid. Everything fell into place the moment I saw your face, the blonde hair doing nothing to obscure your identity, as I'm sure my beard did nothing to hide mine. You said nothing, looking down at the broken glass with everyone else then back up to me, seeing me. There was something in your eyes for those moments we saw each other. Seconds. Minutes. You knew and I knew. And I know you are complicit, part of whatever it was that tried to destroy me, to take my life away. You made me love you but you didn't even have to try that hard.

Was it all an act? Quiet times and gentle touches run through my thoughts, moments that were beyond anything needed for your deception, your con job. In drunken isolation I find cracks in your story, things that I ignored at the time that could have brought suspicion, that any of my friends may have raised an eyebrow at if I'd introduced you to anyone. I see now how you avoided ever meeting anyone else in my life, your claims of being a homebody, just wanting to be alone with me. We never went to your apartment, if you even had one. Your job remains a mystery. General office work through a temp agency in buildings downtown, never at one long enough to come home with stories about annoying coworkers or yogurts being stolen from the office refrigerator. I never met any friends of yours. I could just be looking for things I missed, making them up, to confirm my own thoughts, to try you in my own court and find you guilty.

I look in the mirror. My linen suit wrinkled. Beard growing too ragged. I barely recognize myself. I miss my round belly and pale skin and my favorite T-shirt bought at a concert in college that you hated. Why did you care? I want to be home, buying groceries and teaching classes, stopping for coffee and doing laundry. I need the mundane, the unexciting, the expected. When that was my life I was fine. There was routine. Everything was in its place. Seconds went by in silent countdown to an eventual death.

Tic.

Seventeen-minute drive to campus in the morning.

Toc.

Three hours of writing in the afternoon.

Tic.

Two hours of television to dull my brain at night.

Toc.

Six minutes to jerk off in the glow of the Kohl's sign coming around the edges of the overpriced blackout blinds I'd bought, and another hour getting to sleep wishing for a more exciting life.

I've experienced exciting now. I'm done with it. Fuck excitement, fuck Pippo, and fuck Olivia. Another bottle of wine done. One more left before I have to go back to the shop at the end of the street to restock.

Glass poured.

Drink.

In front of the mirror again, I laugh at myself.

"Who the hell are you?"

I don't reply, only looking back with the same irritated and drunken glare, a bully staring at someone I find weaker, vulnerable.

This damn suit. A child's costume. I've been pretending to be someone else. Worldly. Exciting. Important. I'm as guilty of pretending as Olivia is. I put the wine glass down and run my hands across the soft material. Fingers go between buttons, and I pull. The threads resist at first, fighting back to remain solid, part of something bigger, until they can't hold any longer.

I rip the shirt apart in front. Buttons fly off. Material tears. My now tan skin shows between the linen curtains that hid my chest. Another pull, the seams along the shoulders give way. I feel my new strength, arms tone and sinewy compared to a year ago when I looked like every other overweight American tourist walking the streets, pointing at everything while wearing an oversized backpack full of nothing that was actually needed for the day.

You're pathetic.

With the leather belt unfastened I let the pants fall to the floor and stand looking at myself in nothing but a pair of black boxers. I feel freed, exposed, open. Hands take in my skin, through the light chest hair, and up to my face, pulling on the long and scraggly beard. Quickly to my suitcase I pull clothes out and drop them on the floor until I find the small case and open it. With the pair of scissors, I start cutting at the beard, pulling more than cutting, the blades too dull for the job. I drop the scissors and grab the electric razor, take the guard off, and run it down the middle of the beard into a reverse mohawk, past the point of recovery, and then move it over my entire face. Black and grey hair flies in the air around me, falls to the ceramic tile floor, coats my sweaty chest, until I am who I once was. Who I was before Olivia. Before Italy.

My face is rough with stubble, the electric tool only doing so much. I go to the bathroom and get my razor from the overnight bag and run the water until it is warm, the hottest it ever gets. No shaving cream, I scrape through the growth, pulling skin along with it. A trail of blood runs down my cheek but I keep going, removing my ridiculous disguise, searching for myself behind the mask. I pause only to take sips of wine, beard hair floating on the top of the beautiful, deep red liquid.

I remove my boxers and stand naked, looking at myself, the me I had pushed behind for what I thought was better, stronger, smarter. I'm done with that person, ready to return to some semblance of normal. Eager to fly home and cook fried eggs every morning and throw my running shoes away in favor of a fucking Big Mac for lunch, eaten in my car while listening to NPR and loving every damn second of it. I feel deprived of my past existence, of my routine, of eating what I want, of more than a year of my life taken by her, in her life and in her death. She doesn't deserve to still be alive. Pippo doesn't deserve to still be walking, strutting around, destroying people so he can drink and party and fuck and fuck *over* whomever he desires.

Stepping into the small shower I turn the water on and the initial blast of cold shakes me, a full shiver down my spine, twisting my neck in the shock. I recover and wait as it warms, then rinse the shorn hair from my skin, running the spray of water across my face, purifying my body, re-baptizing myself to the ordinary, the normal. To the real me.

And they'll do it again.

Through the cleanse I see clearly. For me to ever be complete again, to return to what once was, I see what must happen to them and what I must do. Both cannot exist at the same time. Good versus evil. Light versus dark. I try to remember the verses my mother made me read over and over, but they are gone, another thing forsaken from my former being, my old life.

After the shower I look out the window, standing naked in the floor to ceiling opening four flights above Florence, a million miles from where I should be. I look in my hand at the folded tool, a merger of wood and metal, the two innocent on their own until formed into one instrument. With wet fingers, I pull the blade out of the handle. It is only a pocketknife by design, but open it is long, the blade nearly five inches, long enough to find deep purchase through soft skin and organs. My finger runs down the edge of the blade and leaves an invisible mark so thin that the blood that seeps from it seems to be appearing magically, no opening to have exited my body, and hold my self-inflicted wound to my mouth and taste the blood on my tongue.

My hand goes to the window frame to brace me, unsteady on my feet, as the other hand takes hold of myself as I look down and release the muscles and watch my piss fall four floors to the vacant square.

I finish the bottle of wine while looking out on the city below me, the people beneath me. My skin is still wet as I pull on the clothes of my former self to leave, the wood and metal instrument in the deep pocket of my khakis.

CHAPTER THIRTY-SEVEN

It's the third time I've been so close to Pippo and Scarlet on this trip, that I've worked through a crowd to approach them, to stalk them. Hunt them. And it will be my last. Whatever is going to happen begins here. Ends here. Somehow. My plan is incomplete, diluted with wine and anger without looking three steps ahead. I'm moving my queen with no consideration of my opponent's rook.

They weren't hard to find. The expat bar has specials every Thursday night. Pippo doesn't care about the cheap liquor, just the bigger crowds it pulls in. It provides an audience. Targets, too, perhaps, to milk dry of money. I never found any record of his family name owning a business in Milan, much less one successful enough to provide him with the lifestyle he maintains. That money must come from somewhere, and it is likely from fools like me who fall for the woman that is too good to be true, or perhaps are easily convinced to give their fortunes away if the con fails.

One night at home the memory of the party in Positano tried to pull itself into focus as hard as I worked to push it away. The drugs and wine left those visions blurry at best, pieces missing, gone from my memory, while others are seared in, never to be forgotten no matter how hard I try. It was one of those moments, large fingers on me, a mouth on my skin, others urging me on, hands pushing and positioning me until I gave in to the voices and thrust forward, taking, entering, penetrating. A back arched in front of me, my hands on the hips of tanned Italian skin, a grunt, the cheers around me, and a face turning to look back at me, Vincent, then a flash of light in my eyes.

This is where it began. A table in the corner with Olivia, an abrasive voice in the crowd she pretended to not know while she enjoyed the rude humor and dirty jokes. I shake my head at the thought, antagonized by it. Urged on.

I see them drinking and swaying to the music as they always do. They are snake charmers, hypnotizing their congregation with the seduction of wealth, good looks, and charisma in a one-on-one setting. Influencers with no need for Instagram or YouTube channels, earning their followers in person. Even as a skeptic, knowing the truth about them, I'm pulled in to their movement and have to remind myself of why I am here, of what they have done. Of what I'm going to do.

Olivia isn't with them and I feel a relief in that. I don't know how I'd react if she were. Perhaps she's off on another mission to tear someone apart from the inside, to earn their love and devotion, only to have it betrayed. Instead, Pippo and Scarlet are with another couple. Pippo keeps moving to position himself where the young man can see Scarlet, who plays the part perfectly. The hair toss. The stretching of that glorious neck that had intoxicated me as her hand touches the side of the man's face. All while the young woman falls for Pippo's charm. They look American, at least I want to think they are, that I'm not the only rube from a flyover state to be swindled by them. Without the tunnel vision that had limited my field of view, I see the glances they give each other, unspoken affirmation of targets acquired. It was so obvious now they might as well be lifting wallets from back pockets, pulling out the cash and cards and laughing as they do it.

Pippo's arms are in the air. They're always in the air for some goddamn reason, and I see the watch. His precious Rolex. It truly defines him as a person, gold and shiny but still no different than any other Rolex out there. The watch has bothered me since the first time we met, had drinks after the museum. They told their story about being robbed in the streets of Amsterdam. Phone and wallet taken. But still he has the Rolex. The only thing that could possibly have been sold for real money. The full realization further annoys me that I hadn't placed it before, a tear in the seam of their story, a chink in their armor, the first of many more lies.

How had I missed it? Am I that blind to not have

seen the looks between them, or are they just that good? Another glimpse of Scarlet and my question is answered. With her in view, everything else is ignored. All signs of treachery obscured by her shining hair and radiant skin. It had been the long game. Olivia targeted me thousands of miles away and spent every night with me until the one she faked her own death. That final act with Scarlet outside our bedroom where I took her, held my hand to her throat, a likely distraction while Olivia, alive and well, set the stage for my finding her dead. There were so many signs I should have seen. A beautiful young woman listening to the author of children's mystery novels in a suburban strip mall Barnes & Noble. As with Scarlet, Olivia's smile and never-ending attention to me washed any suspicion away. They gave me the life I thought I wanted all those nights at home before I met them, bathed in filtered moonlight while fighting to get to sleep.

The bottles of wine I drank at the apartment have me thinking slowly, unsure of my movements while too sure of my actions. The double shot of brown Irish liquor I just had from the bar provides false courage, a brief dose of the strength I felt when I was with Sara With No H and her melodic Irish accent. Moments of reason tell me to turn back, grab a taxi, get away from here, fly home. But I don't. I can't. The more I watch Pippo entertain, the more I want to face him, to get revenge. To hurt him. He had hurt me with his game. I had loved like never before and don't know if I ever can again as fully as I had with Olivia. I guess it's easy for her, to make someone love you when you are playing the part to make them fall in love. My words had been highlighted in fluorescent yellow as I read along, falling for every plot twist they devised and orchestrated.

I'm ready, exposed, undisguised. My attempts at being incognito are done. My face once again is as smooth as when they had known me. I look more like I had when I'd made love with Scarlet, and when I did nothing to stop Pippo from touching me, from doing everything he had done that night, from forcing me to fuck Vincent. The drugs had stopped me from saying no to anything, and there was nothing I didn't do. His stink will never leave me and the feel of Vincent in front of me will never go away.

I leave my drink on the bar and move toward them, steps unsteady, weaving through the crowd. I am ready though I don't know what I will do.

My hand grips the knife deep inside my right pants pocket. I purchased it from a shop a block off *Piazza Santa Croce* two days ago. I liked the shape of the wood, the stain bringing out the grain, the contrast of the steel. It was bought as a souvenir, not a weapon; a gift for my father who enjoys sitting outside on warm evenings carving small animals out of wood. I have the blade exposed in my pocket and push it against the outside of my thigh as I walk, a reminder it is there and of what it can do.

For a year I thought Olivia was dead, and for part of that I believed Pippo was involved in her death. I don't know if I can kill him, but in this moment I am sure I can hurt him. My injury had been emotional. His can be physical.

A man bumps into me, spilling from the two glasses of red wine he is carrying onto my shirt, and I stumble left, losing my balance. The edge of the blade goes through the thin lining of my Docker's khaki pocket and deep into my thigh. I feel the warmth of blood on my skin as it flows freely down my leg. The man mumbles obscenities in another language and disappears in the crowd. I'm turned around, off course. I look to obtain my target again. I don't feel my new wound through the drunkenness and don't care about the red wine soaking my shirt, sticking it to my chest. A warm drip down my leg and I glance down to see the dark red blood soaking through the khaki pants. My head spins. I hear Pippo and turn too quickly.

His back is to me and I smell him. His narrow shoulders nearly at my eye level. I bring the knife out and look down at it, a layer of my own blood on the shiny blade. It's appropriate, if not poetic, that our blood will mix when the metal enters him. That a part of me will injure him, as a part of me has been killed by his actions.

I have the knife in front of me, pointed at him, real-izing I don't know how to hold it, how hard it will be to puncture skin, insert the blade. What if I hit bone. Anyone near who looks down would see it. If Pippo were to step backwards he would impale himself with no help from me besides my holding the weapon steady if it didn't collapse in my hand under the pressure, probably cutting me instead. I hesitate. I consider where to place it, where there are no bones to get in the way, where I can do enough harm to injure. Or worse.

I raise my head to look at the back of his, the heavily gelled hair held motionless in his movements. His scent enters my nose and takes me back to the days and nights spent together, drinking and partying, sharing our women and each other. The smell is acrid, a combination of manmade and natural odors combining into something sour. I wish to smell Scarlet, not him. I had run my face across her skin, inhaling her floral essence, her pheromones exotic to my white-bred small town testosterone, bringing something new out of me, something savage. I need that energy now.

My decision is made and I put the knife below his rib cage. The kidneys. Perhaps the liver. Not the heart or lungs. I don't want him to die, not quickly at least. I want him in pain. I want him to see me after. To recognize me and know. I feel the desire for revenge more than I had before. My body moves in time with his, in time with the music, synchronized with the people around us, a constant blur of skin and hair. The point of the blade is at his back, eager to move forth, to taste skin and drink blood. His loose green shirt snags on the sharp point as I push it forward.

A scream explodes across the room and everybody in motion freezes, the music seeming to grow louder in the absence of voices and laughter.

The sound registers once the shock of the moment recedes. It's not a scream of pain but surprise, excitement. I'm confused and lower the blade, holding it against my leg, ready if needed. I look around. Had someone seen me, seen the knife? I move back through the crowd, needing distance, a better vantage point to assess from, to escape if need be.

I realize the scream was the other woman that Pippo was seducing, scamming. She is looking down. They all are now, Pippo and Scarlet, the other couple and those in the close circle around them, standing shoulder to shoulder. Then hands come up from the ground and the others grab on to them, pull them, laughter forming and erupting from the epicenter out through the crowd until people who don't know what is happening are joining in, as a woman in a white dress is brought to her feet in the middle of the gathering. Red hair sweeps over smooth pale shoulders and my heart feels as if it might seize.

"I don't know what happened!" Sara says. Her Irish accent is thicker and words are slurred as she constantly adjusts her feet to maintain balance, hands reaching out to steady herself on any shoulder nearby. A hand falls onto Pippo's chest then pats around as she looks up at him, nearly a foot taller than she.

"Oh my, look at you." It comes out in one long, dragged out brogue of a word, *ohhmyyyloooa'youuu.*

I back away, allowing the crowd to swallow me.

Sara's dress is white and clutches her skin in the right

places and I recognize it. We had seen it in the window of a shop she couldn't afford to walk into, much less buy anything from. She had ooh'ed and ahh'ed the dress and I could feel her melt on my arm for it. "Maybe someday," she said. I thought about buying it for her right then, but it felt too large a gesture for our days old relationship that was closing in on its half-life.

Pippo and Scarlet are holding her arms and from my detached distance I see them both look her up and down, followed by the briefest moment of locking eyes with each other. In that instant, I saw it, the agreement, the confirmation, the cartoon dollar signs in their eyes bulging in and out.

All of their attention was on Sara now. Halfhearted excuses were made, acts of kindness declared as they said they wanted to help her, take care of her, and they escorted her to the door as I followed, allowing several people between. At the door Sara shrieks and yells, pushing away from Pippo and Scarlet as she does.

"Where's my *fecking* purse!"

A white leather clutch that matches the dress is found on the floor and passed through several hands to mine. I glance up at Sara who is looking at me. She winks. I hand the purse to a man between us and turn away before Pippo or Scarlet see me.

The door closes and they're gone.

CHAPTER THIRTY-EIGHT

Florence glows at night as streetlights illuminate the walls and reflect off the ancient stone roads that have been worn smooth over centuries. It's one of many things that makes the city feel magical. Within the city center, the streets are narrow and lined with three and four-story buildings. It can feel claustrophobic if you allow it to be. Even though the structures are nowhere near the height of the towers in New York City, the width of the roads pulls them in on you.

Following someone in a car is hard. One-way roads and construction block you at every turn. On foot, it is much more simple. Footfalls echo as I chase them, but disappear through the streets and alleys, hiding their origin, while I'm trying to stay at a safe distance, all while keeping an eye on Sara. She is still slung between the two of them, supported by them, as they work their way home. They are enamored by her, or at least by the money they think she has. I don't understand what their game is with her, how they would bleed her dry like they did with me. A quick score, perhaps, not a windfall. A few thousand to finance the next adventure, the next meal, or the next night out on the town. I'm not worried about her physical safety. Not yet, at least.

They pass by several taxis, staying on foot. A smart move to avoid having an impartial person involved, someone to overhear a drunk woman's request to go home or witness her resistance to getting out of the car at a building she doesn't recognize, not knowing Sara is far from intoxicated.

I stay far back, having the luxury of knowing where they are going, to avoid being seen or heard. There isn't much I can do except watch from a distance and wonder what they will do with her, what their first step is.

She came out of nowhere at the bar. I was so focused on the couple that I missed her entering, stunning in that expensive dress. When she walked away from me at the café I thought I wouldn't see her again. Maybe that was her plan. But something pulled her back. I don't want to be egotistical enough to think she came back just for me. She had been upset by the stories of Pippo and Scarlet, and the effect seeing Olivia alive had on me.

It's another ten minutes before we get to their street. I pull closer, knowing the doorways I can hide in on this road. It is wider than most and I'm almost across from their apartment by the time they reach the door.

As Pippo is getting his key, Sara slides out of Scarlet's grip and falls to the ground. He gets the door open and helps her up. They are holding her between them again but she's facing backwards, their arms under hers. One of her hands goes to her mouth then drops, grabbing the edge of the door as they pass. The door swings closed, and the clear sound of the wood hitting the frame reverberates down the street.

A light comes on upstairs. Shadows pass the windows. I move across the street, getting to the wall beneath their apartment, out of view if anyone were to look out. Stopping at the door, I glance around, then grab the large metal knob. Before I can attempt to turn it, setting off a lever on the backside that slides the crossbar out of both clasps, the door swings open. I step in and look down at the edge of the door and see a wad of gum stuck into the mechanism. She continues to surprise me.

I pry the wet gum out with my finger so it won't be found later. Inside the first-floor atrium, I can hear voices upstairs in the apartment. Pippo is doting on Sara, flaunting his endless Italian charisma in an attempt to remove panties or debit card PIN numbers from the seemingly drunk woman.

The stairwell curves from the left wall, across the back, then ends twenty feet high on the right at the double door entry to the apartment. It is still open, the heavy wood not swinging shut on its own after they helped Sara in. I take position beneath the stairs, obscured in the shadows, to lie in wait. For what I am waiting, I do not know yet. Sara seems to have led me here and I feel I must trust her.

I never expected to be back in this building. Any thoughts I've had over the months of thinking about them, standing in front of them again, it was never here. This was the inner sanctum. The keep. There are memories of this building I'll never get over. This is where I first saw Scarlet's naked body, across from me pleasuring Pippo, as I lay on top of Olivia. That was the beginning of the fall, where I lost who I thought I was. It all becomes clearer with every memory that floods back, how they had primed me, hazed me. Seduced me. Olivia could have stolen my money any time back home, but I would have known it was her. And for them, it wouldn't have been as much fun. They like to play with their dinner, not eat it quickly.

Sound carries, bouncing off the stone walls, and I hear everything. A cork pops from a bottle, one of his signature moves with an expensive Prosecco from what he claims to be a family vineyard.

"You look lovely in that dress," he says.

"What an amazing apartment." Her words are still slurred. She plays the drunk well. "Look at all these old books. Have you read all of them?"

I imagine where she is, where she's standing, near the ledger and the miniature statue of the Rape of the Sabine Women, a suitable monument to him.

"Come sit with me." His charms are failing against a woman who knows who he is. Scarlet seems to have disappeared, leaving him to seduce.

"You must be rich to have this place," Sara says. "Are you rich?"

"I don't like to—"

"I bet your daddy is rich." Her voice changes volume and tone as she moves around the room. She's not sitting still to let him have advantage, to lay his hands on her.

He sees a chance to impress. "My family lives in Milan and—"

"I haven't been to Milan. Is it nice?"

"It is a beautiful city with wonderful archi—"

"Is this Prosecco?" She gives him no openings, interrupts him at every step.

"Yes, it is from—"

"I can't drink Prosecco."

"I have wine." His voice becomes more heavy, annoyed.

"I mean, it makes me sick."

"Let me get you something el—"

"Oh, *shite.*" The next sounds disgust and delight me as I hear her gagging followed by the liquid discharge of vomit onto the marble floor.

Pippo yells loudly in Italian. Though I don't recognize his words, the translation is international.

"What's happening?" Scarlet's voice.

"This bitch is throwing up everywhere."

"Let's get her cleaned up."

"No, I want her out of here. She's not worth it. Nothing but Irish trash in an expensive dress."

I move farther back into the shadow and stifle a laugh. It was only a minute later that they are helping her down the stairs. Sara is between them, her feet pretending to struggle to find purchase against the stone floor. She doesn't look around for me, but I do see her look at the edge of the door on the way out. The large wood door to the street slams shut. The building is quiet.

I wait in the silence, not eager to enter the apartment above. I want to follow Sara, make sure she is safe, but she did this for me.

Up the stairs two at a time and through the entry to the apartment. Only one light is on in the far corner, casting yellow incandescence that fades to darkness.

I don't think it was ever this quiet in here. Either Pippo was talking or music was playing. There was always activity, white noise.

When I sat at the café with Sara this morning and told her the story from the beginning, she'd been patient, listening to every detail, and asking for more information when she felt there should be more. Things I had missed when they happened. I found clarity in her questions, like a therapist digging into your past, helping you realize for yourself why you don't like sweet potatoes or avoid hugging people.

I told her about the morning we left for Capri. I had awakened hungover from the pills and confused when Olivia was rushing me out the door to some unknown destination. But just before leaving I had seen Pippo with a brown leather ledger, a pencil in his hand.

"It's the money," Sara said. "It's where he tracks his money."

I stared at her, upset I hadn't realized that.

"Are you sure?"

"I'm an accountant. Trust me. I'm sure he takes it with him whenever he travels. I would. I would also keep it in a more secure format than a leather binder."

That was in Positano. Not here. I look around the room. There's a desk in front of the wall of built in bookshelves, a leather blotter and small lamp with a green glass shade on it. I open the single drawer to find only a notepad and some pens.

Rows of books line the shelves, none showing any sign of having been opened. Text on spines is in Italian and look like classics on display for show, not favorites to be thumbed through on winter nights. I see the miniature recreation of The Rape of the Sabine Women, the original, full sized sculpture residing here in the main square of Florence only blocks away. It is his favorite sculpture, as he told us on several occasions. We stopped in front of it on a walk late one night and he grew silent as he took it in, though he lives not far from it. It was the sincerest I had ever seen him, truly humbled by something beautiful.

I move closer to the small sculpture and see a book behind it. Reaching up, I pull out the brown ledger. I flip it open to see page after page of handwritten notes. Names, addresses, and most importantly, numbers. One page alone accounts for over half a million dollars. This can end him. With calls to people listed or photos of pages anonymously released to reporters, his scam will be over.

I close the book and take a last look around. On the bar sits a still sealed bottle of wine I know from a year ago. It was one of the best I've ever had. I head for the door with it under my arm, relieved to have this place behind me, and soon, Florence and all the circles of hell it has brought me.

"Avery?" The voice breaks the silence and I wonder how I hadn't heard footsteps.

I stop, startled, as my stomach wrenches.

"It was you." Olivia says. "At the bar last night."

I let myself look over at her, almost fearful of her for the first time. Of what else she could do to me.

"I'd know those eyes anywhere," she says. "You shaved. You look good."

"Did you tell them you saw me?"

She moves closer and I step back.

"I didn't."

"Why not?"

"I don't know. I tried to tell myself it was coincidence, that you were only here on vacation again. I should have known better."

Again she moves toward me and I hold my ground this time. My eyes are staying below hers as if I think she can turn me to stone if our gazes meet. I just don't want to look into them and risk falling for her once more, find myself believing her lies, craving her lips.

"Why did you come back?"

"I wanted to know what had happened to you," I say. "To…your body."

"It's right here, Avery." Closer, again. The thin nightgown she's wearing hides nothing.

"You look a bit more alive than the last time I saw you."

"I'm sorry. I didn't want to do that to you, but he made me. He makes me do everything."

"What do you mean?"

She turns and takes her first steps away from me. "It's Pippo. I can't…" Her voice disappears.

"You can't what?"

"I can't leave. He owns me."

"What the hell are you talking about?" I say. "What do you mean?"

"He saved me, gave me a second life."

In all the months together, I rarely heard stories about her past, her childhood, and when I did, they were simple, stripped down, void of names and details. She always claimed to be a private person, that pasts didn't matter.

"How?"

"He was…a customer. I was living in Amsterdam, working in a—"

"You were a prostitute?"

She lowers her head and nods, showing or faking shame and embarrassment.

"Three nights in a row he came to me, then asked me to leave with him. So, I did. He showed me a life I never knew was possible." She looks around the room. "I owed him and then he took me over."

"How long have you been with him? With them?"

She considers for a moment. "Two years, I think. Maybe a little longer. At first things were fun. We traveled, drank, shopped. They would disappear for days at a time, once for almost a month. I never asked where they went."

"They were working someone."

She nods. "Later we were in Barcelona. They were quieter than usual. Than ever, really. We sat at tables in clubs instead of dancing and drinking. Scarlet pulled her chair next to mine and pressed against me. That's when she pointed out a man at a table across the room."

"Your first?"

"My first." She considers the past. "It was only a few weeks with him. He was shy, introverted. But once we got close he changed."

"How?"

"He hit me when I was late meeting him one night."

My body heated up in anger thinking about a man from long ago raising a hand to her. I inhale slowly, calming myself, distancing myself. I could be pulled into her so easily.

"What happened?"

"I'm not sure. Pippo sent me home with Scarlet and he arrived back a day later."

"Did he kill him?"

"I don't think so. I don't know."

"What about Vincent?"

"What about him?"

"You didn't hear? His boat blew up, right after I saw Pippo exchange bags with him in the middle of the night."

She stares at me, looking like she is determining if I am telling the truth before allowing it to sink in. She shakes her head slowly.

"I didn't know. Vincent is, was, a good man. He was sucked into Pippo's circle, too. He usually does whatever is asked. They used him for— "

"Blackmail."

She nods. "Pippo hates computers. He barely uses a cellphone. He's always trusted Vincent to keep any photographs that might be needed, somewhere safe, away from here. I overheard them talking about him a few days ago after getting back from a short trip. Something happened and Pippo was upset. More than that. He was screaming at Scarlet out here while I was in my bedroom. He just kept saying that everything is gone."

"What was he talking about?"

"Vincent told me one time he wanted to leave. We were drinking together while Pippo and Scarlet were out of town. He was very drunk and said he had thought about deleting everything, destroying the computer, and disappearing."

"I saw Pippo meet Vincent in Positano a few days ago. They traded bags at the dock."

"That's why he has it. The laptop was here the other day. He must have gotten it from Vincent, but everything was erased."

"And now Vincent is dead."

"I just can't believe that. Pippo has done some horrible things, but kill someone?"

"Could Vincent have faked it? Taken whatever money he got from Pippo and just disappeared?"

"It's possible. Vincent was very broken and getting worse. Pippo's control, it was always mental. He breaks you down. He worked me until I had no fight."

"You never seemed in distress to me."

"Not physically."

She walks past me to the bookshelves. Her hand reaches up and strokes the smooth contours of the sculpture.

"Do you know why it's his favorite?" she says.

"No." My eyes don't leave her, partly in awe of seeing her and partly in fear of her.

"I don't think it's the beauty of the piece at all. He doesn't have that in him." She lifts it with two hands. I can tell the weight it has as she lowers it to look closer. "In early Rome the men became concerned that there were not enough women to enable the society to last. Attempts to attract and even purchase brides failed, so the men went into the area around the city and took women to be their wives in a mass abduction. To be nothing more than breeders to do their bidding. This was called the *raptio*."

She has the smile and glow she always gets when talking about the art, her love of the history, the beauty in the shapes and even the darkness.

"The meaning behind *raptio* then was abduction. Kidnapping. But over the centuries it has taken the more common use of the Latin word. Rape. I always felt the art world used the word to make it more provocative."

"And that's what he did to you, to other women," I say. "He took you."

She nods and places the statue back on the shelf, careful to put it in the same position it had been. "Not as breeders, but definitely for sex. For his enjoyment. For his games to deceive innocent men and women and relieve them of their money."

"Why me? How'd he choose me?"

"He knew who you were before I ever set eyes on you, Avery. How he finds people, I don't know. I've heard him talk about locating men with just enough money to make it worth his time, but not enough they can afford to come after him. 'No millionaires,' he likes to say. And sometimes, it's just people they see at a bar. A quick flip. Scan the credit cards, drain some accounts and move on. But you. He sent me to you. It was something he planned out. It has become a game for him. My job was to make you fall in love with me and bring you here. A play thing."

"It worked."

"Too well. I fell, too."

"I can't believe that, not now."

She looks different. A year has passed, but it's more than that, more than the blonde hair. The way she stands, how she holds herself. Not as confident. Broken.

"Why don't you leave?"

"I can't. You don't know the things he's done. He'd find me. There's been others before me."

"Others?"

"Other women."

"What happened to them?"

"I don't know. They just go away. We're toys for Pippo and Scarlet."

"You could have run. All those months with me, you could have told me. I would have protected you."

She shakes her head. "No. He would have found me. I was never totally alone. Whenever I wasn't with you, I was with him or one of his other women, always there to check on me, keep me on task."

"What about Scarlet?"

"It's different with her. She has a way of controlling him, influencing him, maybe. She acts all sisterly to me, but also makes sure I don't start taking too much of his attention. In a way she's protective of him, but that makes sense since without him she's nothing."

I take in her every move, her expressions. I find no reason to think she's lying, but none to say she isn't. She's blank.

She looks at the ledger in my hand. "You know what that is then?"

I nod.

"You can destroy him with that."

"I know."

"Will you?"

"I don't know yet. Everything I thought I came here to do, the reasons behind it, the months of mourning for you and missing you, were destroyed last night when I saw you. What they did to me...it means nothing now. I don't care. I just don't care about them anymore."

She steps closer, close enough she could reach out and touch me, but she doesn't. I can smell the lotions that still linger on pillows back home, on my memory of holding her and loving her. That sweet scent had been so strong in the downpour of rain in San Gimignano when I held her from behind and watched the storm move slowly over us.

Without seeing her move, her hand is on my arm, her skin on mine for the first time in a year. I feel her warmth and let it soak through me and want more, want all of her, to forgive her and take her away with me.

She squeezes, her thumb stroking my skin.

"Can I find you after, if I'm still able to?" she says.

Long nights of holding her, making love to her, being comfortable with her are still fresh in my mind, having been dreamt of so many times since losing her. Seeing her now only strengthens the memories. I spent so long wanting to grab her and hold her again and hope that things could be how they were.

"No."

CHAPTER THIRTY-NINE

The square below is empty and silent. Any sound would echo and travel up through the open window, but there is none. At this hour there are no cars, no tourists. I keep the lights off and stand where I can see through the break in the curtain while hidden in the dark, down the forty feet to the street, surveying the area.

My dad built me a treehouse when I was about ten, much to my mother's argument against it. It wasn't much more than a wooden platform perched on some branches with three boards nailed to the trunk to climb up. No roof or shelter of any kind, as much as I wished to spend nights out there alone. It was freedom, solitude. Independence at eight feet high. I would sit there for hours, reading or watching the world that seemed so far below, even though to get down I would only have to grab onto one of the supporting branches, swing, and let go to fall to the ground. One day I sat on the edge of the platform, legs dangling, mind wandering. It was an especially hot day in Kansas with no breeze. Everything was still, silent as it is before a tornado, but the skies were clear and sunny. My thoughts went to the upcoming school year, girls I liked, and all the other things a young boy thinks about as I grew tired in the heat, eyelids heavy and wanting to close.

My eyes opened and I was lying on the ground below the simple treehouse. I wasn't awakened by the fall. Somehow, I just fell and continued sleeping. I remember wondering what my mother would have done if she had looked out the kitchen window and seen me face down on the ground, so I stayed there, waiting to see. But she never came running out of the house screaming. Later, when I went inside, she was sitting at the table going through mail and without even looking up, said, "You fall out of that tree?" I mumbled *Yes ma'am* and went on to my room.

When I left their apartment an hour ago, I took a taxi and directed it the wrong way, watching behind as the small car maneuvered through the tight streets, before giving a location closer to home. The driver acted annoyed but the fare kept climbing. I had him drop me several blocks from my apartment. On foot, I worked back and forth through the dim yellow lights, backtracking and circling buildings to make sure nobody was following. I don't know if I'm being paranoid or cautious.

From the shadow of a building across the square I had watched my apartment windows and the door four floors below for ten minutes before approaching while holding the leather book tightly with sweaty hands. My thoughts worked through what might happen when Pippo and Scarlet return home from getting rid of the woman they thought only to be a sick drunk. I don't know if Olivia would give me away, tell them the moment they walk in that I had been there, that I had taken the ledger. Would she slam her face into a wall to bloody and bruise herself to look like I had beaten her up, taken it by force, upset at being rejected? Or did she go back to bed and lie there looking at the blank ceiling as she listened to them work their way through the apartment until they go off to their own bedroom? Whatever happens, the missing ledger will be discovered before long and I plan to be nowhere near this city.

Sara. Through all the lies I told her, in words and omission, she came. She must have followed me, or perhaps them. It was beyond anything I would have imagined, or anything I would have agreed to. One final act for a stranger in another country, an accidental lover. Perhaps when time has passed and everything has settled I'll try to find her, somehow. A note to thank her, tell her I'm okay, and ask if she is.

I leave the lights off, not ready for the brightness. My torn linen shirt is on the floor. Back in the shower I wash myself for the second time tonight, now sober and muscles sore. My hand runs gently over the cut in my leg from the sharp knife, blood still oozing slowly when pressed. I clean the wound as well as possible through the pain and after the shower wrap it with a hand towel, a makeshift bandage for the night. The cut needs stitches, but I'm not going to a hospital, not now, not here. I'll keep it clean and closed as well as possible until I'm back home.

I check all the wine bottles, but they're empty except the one I took from Pippo's apartment. The cork comes out easily and I pour it into a wine stained glass. I don't want to be drunk again, just numb from the pain on my leg and from seeing Olivia, feeling her hand on me.

Sitting on the end of the bed, I flip through the ledger until I find my name. *Hinton Chase* is written across the top, then crossed out and replaced with *Avery Gross* beside it and I let out a laugh. He hadn't even known my real name when he picked me. The notes read like a mortgage application. Bank account numbers and balances at the time, social security number, credit card numbers and PINs to go with them. My email address and password. Olivia had done her job well.

Every page is a history of deceit, of people losing their life savings so one man can do whatever he wants. I wonder how many of them know who stole their money, who were blackmailed with illicit photos taken during drug fueled orgies, or if some don't even care, happy to have had the attention for a short while and rich enough to lose a hundred grand or more. Certainly, someone's pieced together the puzzle and has plans for revenge. The book I hold is everything they would need, but it feels wrong in my hands. The energy I had to find them is gone.

I get a glass of water from the bathroom sink and after drinking it all realize how dehydrated I am and pour another. I throw the linen shirt in the trash. The suit pants are wrinkled and dirty, but salvageable with a good dry cleaning back home, so I wad them up and put them in the suitcase along with the jacket and the rest of my belongings. I want an early start, earlier than I know Pippo to ever wake. The first train is at 5:45 and I'll be on it. I leave my shorts and T-shirt out to travel in and pack everything else to grab and go.

Once I let my brain think about sleep my body follows suit and the exhaustion from the night catches up with me. Sitting on the edge of the bed in my boxers I glance over for one last night view of the *duomo* from my window. The light on the red terracotta tiles glow for one last bit of magic. A part of me will miss this place. Even through the bad things.

I'm leaving tomorrow. The Florence airport is too obvious, too close. My open-ended ticket has been rebooked. I have to avoid using my credit card, in case Pippo still has visibility into my accounts, change passwords again, change everything. I want to be back in my own home, the ordinary surrounding me. The memory of Olivia will still be there, but it will be different now. I won't be missing her like I had. Pillowcases can be washed to remove the last olfactory traces of her. She said Pippo had been there to watch over her at times. In Kansas. Near my home. The thought of him being able to find me so easily hadn't crossed my mind.

Three light taps. I barely hear the knocking. My heart beats louder than the sound so I am unsure if there is another as I step to the door. There is no peephole.

I stand away from the center, by the frame, as I see people do in movies when worried about being shot through the door in a heightened sense of fear.

I whisper. "Hello?"

A whisper back. "It's me."

Sara.

I reach for the doorknob, then hesitate, no way of knowing if she's been followed, or they forced her to bring them to me. I grab the ledger and look around the room, then slide it between the dresser and TV stand. Back to the door, I turn the knob and pull it open a few inches. I see Sara, alone, in pants and a dark blouse, a large hat hiding half her face. The white dress is gone.

"You alone?"

"Of course I'm alone."

I open the door and let her in, stepping out to the landing to look down the stairs before going back in and closing, then locking the deadbolt.

I turn and she is on me, arms around me, face nuzzled into my neck and I hold her as I feel her body begin to vibrate and she cries.

"Are you okay? Did they hurt you?"

Her head shakes "no" on my shoulder. She leans back and I see her face. Through the tears she is smiling and laughing.

"I was so scared," she says. "But it was so exciting and frightening and crazy."

"I can't believe you." I pull her warm body against mine and feel complete and cry and laugh with her.

"Did you get it?" Her voice is soft with her face against my chest.

"I did."

"Is it what I thought?"

"More."

CHAPTER FORTY

Sara sleeps naked beside me, the soft white sheet loose over her body. Occasional tiny sighing exhalations and what sounds like a giggle. It's nice. Comfortable. To occupy space with another person and not feel claustrophobic is about all a person can ask for. Perhaps that's the meaning of life, that comfort. To find the one you can be with that their sounds don't annoy you.

My parents revolve around each other in silent circles, never touching unless behind a closed bedroom door. But they are happy and always were when I was young. I rarely saw them disagree and don't recall them ever fighting. But there weren't signs of affection. I've never seen them kiss or cuddle. It affects a child, their perception of what a relationship is, what love is, what caring is.

Though exhausted, my mind is in motion, churning away at the unknown. I'm trying to analyze messages that are coming from within my own psyche. They emanate from deep inside, full of static and unclear, congregating in my waking thoughts and making me delirious. I don't know if it is things I've missed, clues left behind that will point them to me, to harm me, to harm Sara, perhaps. Or is it just the past haunting me? Not allowing me to rest even as I prepare to leave. Whenever I think of the ledger and what to do with it, the feeling is stronger, dizzying.

Nothing remains but my escape, the final exit from this city, and that is booked in first class on Lufthansa tomorrow.

If Olivia doesn't tell them I was there, I don't know how long it will be before he notices the ledger missing. I saw him writing in it only once. It could be days. A week, perhaps. At that point would Olivia give me up, confess to what had happened, tell them about watching me leave with the book. Would he hurt her? Would he kill her? I try to act disturbed, frightened at the thought, but can't. They know where I live if she does tell. I'm easy to find.

Or perhaps he'll discover it missing and think first of the drunk Irish woman, the last stranger to enter their castle. Would they go to St. Regis Hotel where they left her, where she said she was staying, and sit in the lobby watching for her, pressuring bellboys and the housekeeping staff for information on the Irish redhead in the white dress?

I held Sara in my arms earlier. We talked about what has happened and what comes next. I have no answers.

This is uncharted territory on an ancient map. *Here be dragons.*

"You're going home?"

"Yes."

She became quiet. Her hand on my chest fell still. I could feel the sadness but didn't know if it was hers or mine.

"What if I came with you?"

The thought had been running through my mind since she appeared at the apartment late last night and still is as she sleeps beside me. Our relationship, if you can call it that, is in its infancy, propped up by the drama surrounding me, the excitement, the danger. She chose to get involved, surprising me at the restaurant last night, allowing herself to be taken into their lair so selflessly.

"You would want that?" I say. "What about your job?"

"I can find a job in Los Angeles."

Oh, the lies I have to come out from under. They are weighing me down. But I didn't tell her. I couldn't. I'm still in self-preservation mode.

Her breathing beside me is steady. It calms my nerves in its repetition, the soothing and almost imperceptible motion of the bed. The weight of a body beside you. I want to sleep. At the same time, I want to remember everything and forget it, put it away, behind me.

The ledger is sitting on my suitcase a few feet away. It was never my intended end of the journey, the prize of this self-imposed mission. Over the final hours this leather-bound book forged itself as the symbol of victory. And now I don't know what to do with it. There's enough information in it to stop Pippo, to bring him down, whatever that might mean. Copies of pages could be sent to the names written inside, letting them know what happened to their money. It could be turned over to law enforcement. It could be thrown in a fire and burned. After thinking about all the possibilities, I realize mostly that I just don't care.

The story I had to tell ended when I saw Olivia alive. Speaking to her the next night only provided the conclusion. All I wanted was answers and they came along to the beat of an indecipherable song, the rhythm playing out, beat by beat, over my time back in Italy. Our relationship was already over, but I had mourned her death for a year and needed to know more. There was no closure, no funeral, no body to cry over. No one to talk to. It drove me crazy and it pulled me back here.

Rejecting her last night wasn't difficult. There is no *us* anymore. She guaranteed that with her death and resurrection. Nothing will make up for that.

As the hours wear on me and sleep comes, final waking thoughts are formed and considered. Some are pushed away. Others are pulled forward. Polished. To put this behind me, I know what I have to do.

CHAPTER FORTY-ONE

The airport is a sudden return to reality with no grace period. Back to normal after the illusion of Florence and Positano, the pleasure of Sara beside me in bed. At a glance I could be anywhere. New York. Paris. London. Tulsa. Dingy white hallways filled with people miserable from traveling. The smell of jet fuel fumes. And the ever-present hint of old cinnamon. I'm happy to be here, ready to get home, to feel normal again.

I remain seated through the final call for my flight. There is still a long line of people waiting to have their boarding passes scanned, allowing them to walk down the jetway and wait some more while passengers find what is left of overhead baggage space. The monotony of air travel.

I slept through most of the train ride to Rome. The excitement of seeing the countryside fly by outside is gone. Sleep came easier than it did while in bed, watching the clock, thinking about what was to come, after wheels leave the ground, Italy behind me forever.

I look left down the hall and see a floral print dress. It moves with each step causing flowers to overlap, hiding and showing again like some mystical garden. Closer now and the detail in the print shows clearly, the brightness of the colors. It's intoxicating and I want to be wrapped up in the pattern. I look up to her face and the glare coming back toward me from staring at her. The woman passes by pulling a carryon bag and talking on her cellphone in a foreign language. German, I think.

I feel no guilt for my choice, only sadness. From the moment it came I knew it was right, what had to be.

The line has dwindled and I step to the end. I could have boarded with the first group, but I hate walking past the privileged in first class, their extra wide leather seats and complimentary champagne taunting me, and don't want to do that to anyone else. It's a luxury I can afford, though I've never chosen it before. For years I drove around the Midwest, pushing back on my publisher who wanted me to travel more, only doing so when I had to go to New York for meetings.

I'm carrying nothing. My suitcase is below me somewhere in the airplane's hold. The pocketknife is wrapped up in a sock and stuffed inside an extra pair of shoes that I brought but never wore. I bought the knife for my dad, but it will stay with me now. It's tied to something darker than it was ever intended to be used for.

The window seat beside me is empty, the belt crisscrossed on the leather and a blanket wrapped in a plastic bag.

I'm offered champagne. *No thank you.* What am I supposed to be celebrating? That I can afford a nicer seat? That we are about to be pummeled through the air at 500 miles per hour? That I'm breathing the same recycled air as everyone else on board for seven hours?

But maybe I am celebrating. It's the end of my story, or at least this chapter. Italy will disappear below the clouds soon, as will Pippo and Scarlet, closing the cover on the demented storybook. I'll spend no more sleepless nights thinking about them. I can't ever remove them from my history, but I don't have to relive my days, and nights, with them. I am sure they will come to mind at times, more at first, then less and less as months pass.

With a thud the door is closed. Flight attendants go into action to do their preflight jobs. It isn't long until the first surge of the giant plane as it backs away from the gate.

I reach into my pocket and pull out a piece of paper and unfold it. Handwritten lines of numbers go from top to bottom and around to the other side. At the top is my name. The left edge is ragged from where I'd torn it out of the ledger.

Sara never stirred when I got out of bed and finished packing this morning. Her sighs confirmed that. So much of me wanted to bring her. We could have explored our relationship and seen if there was something real to it, at a minimum having a lot of fun doing so. But somewhere around 4:00 a.m., I realized she was a part of the past. I couldn't fully leave them behind and still have her. That would be egotistical, narcissistic. We are together only because of them. I was at that restaurant where we met because I was reliving moments with Olivia. Through most of our time together she knew nothing of Pippo and Scarlet, but it was only because of them I was there. I hope she'll understand. I left her once already with no plans to come back. This time would just be permanent.

I left the ledger on the end of the bed, except for the page in my hand. It, too, remains in my past. I don't need it or any of the information inside. My narrative is coming to a close. Perhaps hers was just beginning with that dinner where we met.

Inside the ledger I left a note.

> *I care about you deeply, sweetly, lovingly. Your smile and strength helped me through these final days in Italy. For that I can never thank you enough. Take this ledger and do with it as you see fit. You know better what to do with this information than I do. I need nothing from it, nothing from them. I got everything I needed, and more.*

The airplane banks sharply away from the mainland, out over the sea. I don't look out the window. I don't need to.

CHAPTER FORTY-TWO

Six Months Later

The ocean air invades my nose and lungs. I inhale deeper as I enjoy the saltiness against my skin as I run up the last hill. My breathing is heavy, but strong. The crashing of the waves below me at La Jolla Cove are soothing in their violence, slowly wearing away at the rocks and sand, marking time with each eroded layer. I punch a code into the keypad to open the gate to the building. I jog through and let the gate swing closed again on its own. I take the stairs instead of the elevator, three flights up.

The room is bare inside my condo. No sofa or chairs yet. A small folding table I use to eat on. I left or sold most of my possessions back in Kansas. Fresh start. Clean slate. All the clichés.

When I arrived home from Italy and stepped into my house it didn't feel like home anymore. It was cold. Unused. Inadequate. I walked through each room, beds and chairs that don't get used. A television in a guest room that had never been turned on. It felt like I was walking through someone else's house, someone else's life. It may have been me a year ago, even two weeks ago, but it certainly isn't me now.

Then I made the decision within seconds. There had been no thoughts of it before, no weighing options or pros and cons or even thinking of where I'd want to move. I called a realtor the next day and the property was listed by the end of the week. Shortly after that I was driving to the west coast looking for a new place to live. Travel had shown me life doesn't have to be sedentary. I don't have to pick one place and live there forever. I can move, then if I don't like it, move again.

The experiences in Italy were ones I never expected. There's no way I could have. They were beyond anything I thought possible, good and bad. I found pleasures I didn't know I enjoyed and pain that reshaped me as a person.

It's the smallest unit in the building, but it is all I need. One bedroom big enough for a king size mattress, one bath with a huge shower, and secure parking. The mortgage payments are manageable if I keep churning out kid's mysteries and parents keep buying them. Best of all I have a view of the ocean. My desk is set up in front of the windows that cover the back of the unit and I sit there and write every evening as the sun moves farther down toward the horizon, kissing it, and being absorbed into the ocean. I made a promise to myself not to grow complacent, immune to the view. If ever I find myself not doing a double take or getting lost staring out the window, I don't deserve to live here, to possess this small vista. When I am sitting at my desk there is no place I'd rather be.

I head to the shower and hear the ping of a new email from my computer, as if it knew I were passing by, going somewhere other than my keyboard. Stripped down I step into the water and soak my sweaty skin in the large walk-in. The condo is luxury in pint size, finishing touches suitable for a much larger home. I had more space than I needed in my two story, four-bedroom house in the suburbs. I would spend entire weekends cleaning. Here I've opted for an elderly lady named Gladys who cleans most of the units in the building every other week.

There's still the mundane here. The errands. Buying groceries. Going to the post office. Filling the car with gas. But I don't mind them anymore. They are the normal I need. My milestones to move through the day. I find that nothing is as boring when there are palm trees around. I can walk out of my building and be sitting on a bench over the water in a matter of minutes. I quit teaching and concentrate on my books full time now. Maybe I'll write the great novel I've always wanted to. Maybe not.

I dry off in my bedroom and see the pocketknife. It sits on the dresser as if that's where knives belong. I haven't opened it since the night I held it to Pippo's back. My blood still stains the metal hidden inside the wood. It's the closest thing to a weapon I've ever owned. The linen suit jacket and slacks are in the closet. They've been dry cleaned and pressed, hanging there waiting for an occasion to wear them. I've separated those items from my past even though they come firmly from that other world. The knife is a reminder of what I almost did to another human. It would have been an inexcusable act no matter what had been done to me. I have spent many nights analyzing the madness that engulfed me, took me over to seek answers when what I really wanted was revenge. The suit, well, it just looks good on me.

Shortly after I settled in here, which involved unpacking maybe a dozen boxes and setting up the new bed I bought locally and had delivered, a small package arrived from my parents. I opened it and sat staring at the contents. The Tiny Jesus my mother would touch and pray to daily, her gateway to the rapture. It looked more frail than I remembered, never having seen it anywhere other than mounted on the hallway wall. A short note said I would need it in Godless California. My father used to joke there was no religion west of the Rockies. He had spent time not far from here when in the Navy as a teen, and that was about all he knew about the west coast. It just isn't Kansas, the Bible Belt, where every other corner has a church and steeple, complete with a sign at the street displaying messages updated weekly to inspire you to greater levels of holiness or guilt.

It was easy to leave my lifelong home behind. After

traveling overseas and experiencing more than I ever thought possible, the change was simple. Two weeks were spent driving along the west coast. I stayed a few days in Santa Barbara, and one in Venice Beach. After the drive down to San Diego and La Jolla, my decision was simple.

The people are friendly here without needing to know everything about you. Casual conversations in grocery store checkout lines. Nods and a nice 'good morning' as you pass people on the sidewalk. A few wild nights after swiping right.

I go to my desk and sit down. One new email. I click.

An article from an Italian news website pulls up. I can pick out a few of the words in the oversized headline and the text below on the busy page covered with advertising, but my attention is drawn quickly to the image at the top of the story.

It's him. Pippo.

I find the drop down to change languages and the page converts to an English translation.

Florence Man Wanted for Fraud

Giuseppe Rizzo, also known as Giuseppe Romano and Pippo Giordano, is being sought by the *Guardia de Finanza* for questioning in an expansive case of fraud over the last ten years. Nearly a hundred handwritten pages were anonymously released online with detailed information about victims of his crimes, including names, dates, and amounts stolen. Authorities estimate he has acquired in excess of 13.6 million euro from more than three dozen individuals. He was last seen in Florence with an unidentified woman.

He's younger in the photograph which looks like it came from his passport. His hair was shorter then. He looked simple, plain, honest, and I wonder if it is from a time before he began his deceptions. I stare at it after finishing the article, trying to find what to feel about him, and there's nothing. He is in my past. Scarlet doesn't even earn a mention. Maybe that wasn't her real name, either. Somehow, I've kept their acts separate in my mind, allowing her some level of innocence, though I know she wasn't.

I go back to the email. It came from the contact form on my Hinton Chase website. No name was entered. No reply-to email address given. Sara never knew of my pseudonym or my books. Olivia did. Perhaps this is her way of letting me know she's safe now.

I thought I saw her one day recently. A woman walking down the sidewalk. A flash of brown hair in my periphery while driving. A subliminal vision of her face in the blurred motion. I glanced then looked away again, not wanting to know, not needing to know.

Now before me I have evidence of both of them still caring about me, or at least thinking of me. Sara had posted the ledger online and Olivia likely forwarded me the article. There was no one else who would have. Scarlet, perhaps, but I find that far more unlikely. She is probably on the run with Pippo. New names, new cities, new victims. I'm not scared anymore, but precautions have been taken. Any published addresses for me are to a post office box in Manhattan. The condo was bought through a company I created with my mother's maiden name as the owner.

It's impossible not to change in some ways after going through events like I did. They may not be huge or life changing, but can have an effect on how you see things around you. I don't believe in coincidence anymore. I'm less trusting of new people I meet, but also don't want to be isolated. I chose the condo so there would always be people nearby. A level of security. I'm not acting paranoid, just safer.

After returning home, I tried to write about what had happened, changing names and locations where I could. With each word written I found more signs I'd missed. Everything I put down seemed too unbelievable, that no protagonist could be so gullible to fall for their tricks, their seduction. I found no pain or embarrassment in recalling the stories. I've come to terms with it, accepted it as a part of my past and am leaving it there, behind me. Some of it will fade and disappear, to maybe be brought to mind while watching a movie or when a song comes on in a restaurant. I may look kindly on it at some point, a time of exploration and fun. I put that writing away and haven't returned to it.

The afternoon sun comes over the building and changes the light outside the windows. It's my alarm. Time to sit and write, to find that pure voice for a child to read, the innocence I lost and am still working to find again.

Every once in a while, I look out the window from my desk and think of the day standing at the top of Capri, staring down at the water and all of the boats that seemed like toys from a distance. That moment stood out even at the time as significant. It was the furthest away from myself I thought I could ever be. There are a few other memories I haven't let go of, either.

You can't truly forget Florence once you've been there in love.

The more a thing is perfect,
the more it feels pleasure and pain.

- Dante Alighieri, *Inferno*

Thank you to Alessandra Mezzetti for assistance with Italian translations.

A special thank you to friends, colleagues, and distant Facebook contacts who assisted me greatly by being beta readers for *The More a Thing is Perfect*, and may never look me in the eyes again after having done so.

Wyatt Akins
Tracy Brown
Steve Fox
Ed Hutchison
Mary Kauffmann
Shea Megale
Steve Moriarty

www.ingramcontent.com/pod-product-compliance
Lightning Source LLC
Chambersburg PA
CBHW061602190726

48288CB00007B/2145